Tabby was growing very tired of accusations. "Did I think you'd listen, I might try and change your mind—but the effort would obviously be a waste of my time!"

Vivien wished very much to believe her; and he wished as well not to be made a fool a second time. There was only one way he knew to test a female's true feelings. "What a coil this is!" he groaned, and drew Tabby into his arms.

It was a lovely kiss. The second was no less excellent, nor the third. Tabby's emotions were truly in turmoil now. So well had she enjoyed Vivien's embraces that she had briefly forgotten he believed her to be a demirep. . . .

OUR TABBY

Maggie MacKeever

FAWCETT CREST • NEW YORK

Chapter One

The russet rooster surveyed his kingdom. The warm summer sun beamed gently down on chestnut coppice and neat hedgerow, hop-yard and barn, country house and cottage, corn mill and church. Riotous blooms twined along fences and stiles, beneath a sky of unclouded blue. Plump sheep and cattle munched lush meadow grass. In all, 'twas a picture pretty enough to pluck at any but the most jaded heartstrings, rural tranquillity perfect in every detail, including the rooster's harem clucking and sunning themselves beside a weathered wooden fence.

And then, around a distant bend, rattled a job-coach. It was drawn by nags that suffered greatly in comparison with the well-fed cattle that grazed thereabouts. Offended by the intrusion, the rooster drew himself up majestically and waddled to the edge of the road to survey the approaching coach. One astute glance led him to the conclusion that the job-horses were as short on nerve as on flesh. He awaited his moment. The job-coach drew nigh. The rooster took a deep breath, then erupted in an explosion of feathers and cockcrows beneath the near leader's startled nose. The outcome was inevitable. The frightened nags bolted, not to be brought under control again until the job-coach collided with a low-branched tree, tumbling its sole passenger into a ditch.

"Hang it!" cried Miss Tabitha Minchin, as she thus descended abruptly and painfully into a dry summer's accumulation of dust and dirt. Then she flushed guiltily. Miss Minchin's speech had been unfortunately influenced by the young gentlemen under her uncle's tutelage. She gingerly inspected herself for damage and found none, save for the quantities of nature's bounty with which she was now festooned. Ineffectually, she brushed herself. Then she contemplated the verge of the ditch and was somewhat disconcerted to find herself eye to eye with a vengeful-looking russet rooster. Tabby flapped her hands at it. "Shoo! Do go away, you silly fowl. Oh, Mr. Coachman! Do you think you might help me out of this ditch?"

The coachman's response was eerily disembodied, as well as brief and to the point. "No," he said. "I've got my hands full here, miss. I don't reckon to be chasing my nags all about the countryside."

In response to the man's rudeness, Tabby bit her lower lip. Much as her circumstances had changed of late, she had never before suffered so keen an awareness of just how far she'd come down in the world. Well, she could hardly stay in this ditch in hope that some Good Samaritan would arrive on the scene and nobly overlook the fact that she was a mere hired servant. Tabby eyed the side of the ditch. She had been a tomboy in her youth, which, at twenty years of age, lay not that far in the past. Tabby shooed away the rooster, less hostile now than outright curious. She took a deep breath, hoisted up her skirts, and climbed.

The scene that greeted Tabby on her emergence from the ditch did not elevate her spirits. Even to her inexpert eye it was evident that the job-coach had suffered severe damage to one of its wheels and would travel no farther for a while. "What am I to do?" she cried. "I'm expected in Brighton today. If I'm late, I don't know what will become of me!"

The coachman glanced over his shoulder at his rumpled and distinctly grimy passenger. Nothing in his expression indicated compassion for the plight of the niece of a deceased, and unfortunately impecunious, Cambridge don. "You may as well make up your mind to being late, then, miss," he said, not without satisfaction, because he resented her lack of concern for his own plight. The coachman had his own living to think of, and a broken wheel, and these stupid horses that still hadn't recovered from their fright. But Tabby looked so woebegone that he relented. "Mayhap the wheel's not so bad as she looks. There's a blacksmith shop hereabouts. And an inn." He pointed down the road. "Along there a ways. You go on and see if they can't put you up for the night."

For this night and how many others? Mentally, Tabby counted the little bit of money in her purse. Since there seemed little point in arguing with the driver, Tabby retrieved her portmanteau from the stricken coach and set off down the dusty road. She reminded herself that her new employer had arranged for her transportation and therefore shouldn't be out-of-reason startled to discover that the rickety coach had broken down. One thing was certain: If the tenor of her trip thus far was any indication, Tabby needn't expect any special treatment in her new position as governess to the daughters of Sir Geoffrey Elphinstone.

The summer sun beamed gently down upon field and flower; birds sang and bees droned. It was a scene which had of late enchanted many city dwellers, there being a pugilistic encounter taking place in the neighborhood. So far were Tabby's heartstrings from being touched by the bucolic beauty of her surroundings that she scowled ferociously at a friendly butterfly. It must not be deduced from this that Tabby's disposition was disobliging. In general, Tabby was held to be a pretty-tempered little soul, and under better circumstances she might have enjoyed this

3

outing very well, indeed. But her portmanteau was heavy, and her mourning clothes were hot, and Tabby was uncomfortably aware that there was a blister rising on her heel. She was additionally aware that she was in a dreadful pickle. She must get to Brighton. Perhaps there would be some sort of conveyance for hire at the inn. Tabby envisioned a bustling inn yard, with ostlers and waiters, chambermaids and boots and grooms bustling to and fro. Perhaps she might be fortunate enough to secure a place on the Brighton Mail. But mail-coach passage was even dearer than a stage, and surely one had to make reservations in advance?

Again Tabby mentally counted the scant coins in purse. They would not be enough to purchase even an outside seat. She must wait for the surly job-coachman to come back for her. If ever he did! Oh, what a wretched fix this was. Tabby blinked back tears as she thought of her gay and somewhat feckless uncle, so recently deceased of a putrid sore throat, which had resulted from a schoolboy's practical joke involving a rope ladder and a tub of cold water. How he would scold her for wallowing in self-pity. Tabby squared her shoulders and set off at a brisk if limping pace, a brave little figure in dusty black, wearing a crushed bonnet and hugging her battered portmanteau. Behind her, at a discreet distance, trailed the russet rooster, as if he felt in some degree responsible for her plight.

Chapter Two

The inn toward which Miss Minchin so resolutely plodded lay over the crest of a hill, around a curve. The chain of its weatherbeaten sign creaked in the gentle summer breeze. Tabby would not find it as she anticipated, abustle with yard boys and waiters, chambermaids and boots. No ostlers and grooms darted about the inn yard, soothing impatient horses and passengers eager to clamber aboard a coach waiting to depart. This was a small hostelry, with a thatched roof and only one parlor besides the common taproom. But there were crimson curtains in the lower windows, and bright green shutters, and snow-white window hangings in the bedchambers above.

Judging from the number of raised voices issuing from the bar-parlor, many a weary traveler had found the little inn a welcoming sight. Or, rather, many a sporting gentleman, for the conversation was all of the pugilistic encounter that had taken place in the neighborhood earlier that day. To spare the sensibilities of the female reader—who must shudder at the notion of two modern-day gladiators, stripped to the waist, assaulting each other with naked fists, dislodging teeth and noses and eyes, delivering short, chopping, crashing blows with the full force of the arm shot horizontally from the shoulder until the muscular

5

torsos gleamed with sweat and blood splattered the grass—
those details will not be repeated here.

Nor did Mr. Peregrine Smithton relish a conversation
that rang with such phrases as "fast on his feet" and "displayed well"—and, alas for Perry's pocketbook, "bellows
to mend after the first onslaught"—as well as similarly
sanguine descriptions of pugilistic encounters of the past.
Mr. Smithton made his way toward the window of the
taproom, flicked an elegant wrist, availed himself of a
pinch of snuff. Peregrine failed to understand why a con-
test between two milling coves was the most popular sport
in the country, with spectators—himself among them—
traveling from miles about to see two bruisers give and
take punishment. This opinion he would hardly air in the
taproom, which resounded so merrily with talk of levelers
and muzzlers, and cross-and-jostle work. But he would
certainly air it to one Vivien Sanders, who was responsible
for Mr. Smithton's presence in this place, when next they
met.

Peregrine glanced irritably out the window, although at
this point he'd given up expecting his friend. The scene of
rural tranquillity that lay beyond the somewhat dirty glass
brought no gleam of appreciation to his eye. Mr. Smithton
was growing deuced bored of rural tranquillity. He was
also growing thirsty. Peregrine looked around for the
innkeeper, but the fellow was nowhere to be seen. Feeling
thirstier by the moment, Perry detached himself from the
window, strolled through the taproom door, down a dark
uncarpeted passageway, and out into the sunlight.

So bright was that sunlight after the dark passage that
Mr. Smithton paused and blinked. Raised voices assaulting his ears put him strongly in mind of his onetime sojourn at King's College, where he had done a little study,
but not much; and had come away with a smattering of
the classics, a fraction of French, an elegant penmanship
that distracted its reader from the eccentricity of Perry's

spelling, and an ability to solve simple sums in arithmetic—an ability that many a dismayed creditor had discovered was insufficiently advanced to enable him to keep abreast of his bills.

"So there you are!" Peregrine ejaculated, as his eyes adjusted to the brightness and the innkeeper came into view. "Begging your pardon—wouldn't wish to interfere—but prizefights are a thirsty business, even for those of us who can't clear a lane of men with our fists!"

This pleasant sally caused the innkeeper—a rotund little man whose plump dimensions and rosy cheeks suggested a partiality to his own ale—to turn to Mr. Smithton with a distracted, harassed air. " 'Tis that sorry, I am, sir! To be neglecting my guests. But this, er, person is wishful of hiring a room and won't take my word for it that there ain't any to be had, and even if there was, that it wouldn't *do*!"

Thus reminded of the witness to his exchange with the innkeeper, Peregrine raised his quizzing glass. He had an impression of a dusty, little, brown-haired chit dressed in black, clutching a portmanteau and wearing a battered bonnet; but his interest was otherwise piqued. "Good Gad, is that a *rooster*?" he inquired.

"Yes, it is a rooster!" responded the young lady crossly. "And I haven't the slightest notion why it is following at my heels like a tantony pig! Perhaps you may intercede for me, sir! The innkeeper says there is no room, but I *must* have a room, because I can walk no farther, and because the coachman will come looking for me here, and if I am not here, then I shall never get to Brighton, and then I will be in the very devil—er, in a very desperate case!"

Mr. Smithton surveyed the rooster and reluctantly abandoned the notion of making his fortune by turning it into a fighting cock. "Don't know why you want to go to Brighton," he said judiciously. "Can't stand the place myself. Cits wishful of taking the water. Prinny. The Pavilion. Ugh!'' It occurred to Peregrine that he was being critical, and he glanced apologetically at the damsel. Her big eyes were fixed on him. She was a taking little thing, he thought, even with the dust smudge on her cheek. If only she didn't stare at a fellow so! ''No need to frown at me that way! Don't mean to offend. Each to his own taste.''

The young lady set down her portmanteau, stared at Mr. Smithton's sandy hair and freckled, snub-nosed face. ''Oh, gracious!'' she said. ''It *is* you!''

Mr. Smithton regarded his elegant sleeve, as if for reassurance, and made a mental survey of himself. Double-breasted coat and tight breeches of fine cloth and tailoring; riding boots that gleamed enviably; tall hat with a curly brim that was very much à la mode; white linen stock wound round his throat and tied in a bulky bow that would have aroused the envy of any acquaintance encountered whilst strolling along Bond Street. Indeed, Peregrine would much rather have been in Bond Street. There no one would accuse him of being someone he was not. Who else could anyone expect him to be but himself? It need not be explained, perhaps, that it was not only Mr. Smithton's pockets that were to let. The innkeeper inadvertently came to his rescue, asking, ''Do you know this young, er, person, sir?''

Did he know the chit? Peregrine was appalled. He cleared his throat, muttered gruffly, ''Ain't much in the petticoat line. Still, there's something familiar—*Do* I know you, ma'am?''

Her cheeks were rosy. ''Gudgeon!'' she said. ''I mean, unless I am very much mistaken, you were one of my uncle's pupils, sir. At King's College. Although you were not such a vision of sartorial splendor then! Goodness, Perry, but you have grown very fine.''

Laggard memory at last awakened, prompted by a certain ironic quality in the young lady's tone. ''Good Gad!

Old Tolly's girl! You're a long way from Cambridge, Miss Minchin.'' Mr. Smithton realized the significance of her mourning dress. "The devil! Old Tolly ain't stuck his spoon in the wall?''

Miss Minchin reflected that Mr. Smithton, whose career at Cambridge had been memorable only for the quality of his pranks, had not in the interim between then and now developed a great deal of tact. Who was responsible for his dressing? He looked half strangled by that absurdly high cravat. But Perry was an amiable soul, as well as an amusing rattle, and Tabby was in need of a friend. Particularly a friend who stood on good terms with this very unaccommodating innkeeper. "I'm afraid, Perry, that my uncle has indeed, er, stuck his spoon in the wall. And I am in a sad pickle because I must go to Brighton today!''

Here the landlord intervened, suspiciously. "You know this young person then, sir? In that case I have to tell you that this establishment don't cater to her sort!''

Her sort? What sort was that? Mr. Smithton was distracted by the rooster, which was attempting to admire its reflection in his shiny boot. Understanding dawned, and Perry blanched. "She ain't my doxy! She ain't anybody's doxy! My word on it!'' he protested, then realized that he might have been a trifle rash. "*Are* you?'' he hissed.

Tabby's lips twitched. "Worse!'' She sighed. "I am a governess, and I am probably about to lose my place. I'll tell you something, Perry: It makes me positively sick of the mulligrubs to be as poor as a church mouse.''

Mr. Smithton could sympathize with this sentiment. Did he not find it nigh impossible himself to be beforehand with the world? Miss Minchin looked pale, he thought. She must be sweltering in those dark clothes. It made a fellow stop and think, old Tolly turning up his toes.

"Tell you what!'' Peregrine said. "You must be feeling

9

peckish. You need some nice mushroom fritters and apple pie and tea.'' He recalled his own thirst. ''Or ale!''

The landlord, who had been following this exchange with interest, interrupted hastily. Although he had decided that this dusty young miss wasn't a bit o' muslin looking to take profitable advantage of the influx of sporting gentlemen into the neighborhood, it was unthinkable that she should appear in the taproom, a woman in the bar-parlor being an outrage on the company and on woman-kind; and the other parlor was filled to the rafters with sporting gentlemen. But if Miss wouldn't mind stepping around the corner, the innkeeper promised to provide her with a suitable repast at a rustic little table set beneath the gnarled branches of an ancient oak tree.

Miss wasn't at all averse, and settled down happily with hot buttered muffins and cold pigeon pie, while the rooster made an equally good meal of the crumbs. Mr. Smithton settled down beside her and frowned. He might have done precious little studying during his brief stay at Cambridge, but he knew up from down. ''See here,'' he said sternly, ''you shouldn't be racketing around the countryside on your own. It ain't the thing. Gives folks a very poor notion, if you know what I mean. But then, you always was a bit of an oddity, even as a brat. Prosing on forever about this and that. Too smart by half, which is a disconcerting thing in a female!''

Miss Minchin choked, perhaps on the notion that Mr. Smithton was qualified to proffer her advice. When she could speak again, she gasped, ''Mrs. Phipps was to travel with me. She was our housekeeper, as you may recall. But she had an accident; it is a very long story!'' She related to Peregrine the saga of the unfortunate Mrs. Phipps's altercation with a marauding neighborhood hound, caught red-handed (so to speak) in the very act of filching a joint from off the kitchen shelf. Mrs. Phipps having an equally strong passion for mutton, a spirited chase had ensued,

10

which led into the scullery, where the maidservant had left off scrubbing the floor to flirt with the apothecary's boy. Mrs. Phipps put a foot in the scrub bucket and sprained her ankle, and the enterprising hound and the dinner joint got clear away.

Miss Minchin concluded the tale and wiped buttery crumbs off her chin. "And so here I am! On my way to Brighton to acquaint Sir Geoffrey Elphinstone's daughters with such tidbits of knowledge that seem appropriate to young ladies of their position in life. Or I *was* on my way until that wretched accident. I had thought to hire a carriage." She sighed. "But I doubt I could afford it. I don't suppose—"

"That I could lend you mine?" Mr. Smithton confirmed the contention of his cronies that he thought more swiftly when his idea pot had been primed with a bit of the grape, or in this case a couple or more tankards of ale. "You're barking up the wrong tree. I did have a rig. Had it this morning, in point of fact. Had it three hours ago! Then I made a little wager. To tell truth, Miss Minchin, I'm all to pieces. In the basket. Run aground."

"Oh!" said Tabby, recalling her uncle's opinion of Mr. Smithton as a shocking loose screw. "How very dreadful for you."

Mr. Smithton grinned. "Don't trouble your head about it! I promise you I shan't. I'll make a recovery. This ain't the first time I've been at point nonplus!" It occurred to him that his companion was in a similar position. Naturally she could not be expected to meet such a challenge with the sangfroid possessed by a man of the world. Poor puss! he thought, as he watched Miss Minchin crumble a muffin for the rooster. What a good sort of girl she was, Mr. Smithton decided. Game to the backbone and full of pluck. What a pity it was that she should be reduced to such straits—set adrift, penniless, to make her way in the world, alone, without family to offer succor or shelter or

11

advice—although in Peregrine's opinion, a female with a classical education was just tempting fate. But old Tolly had been the best of the fellows at King's College, as knaggy an old gager as ever drew breath, despite the bees he had in his head about learning Latin and Greek and Hebrew, divinity and moral philosophy. "Tell you what!" said Mr. Smithton. "Something has to be done about this pickle of yours."

"Oh!" Startled, Miss Minchin dropped the remainder of the muffin to the ground. The greedy rooster speared it on his beak and withdrew with his trophy behind a nearby bush. "Do you think you might help me?"

No such notion had occurred to Mr. Smithton, who was not accustomed to expending energy upon aught but himself. But he was not accustomed, either, to pretty damsels who gazed upon him as if he were a Good Samaritan. This novel experience—and, perhaps, the excellent quality of the innkeeper's ale—recalled to him a circumstance that he had hitherto forgotten.

"Wouldn't say I could if I couldn't!" Peregrine said expansively. "Don't know why I didn't think of it before, except I was so surprised to see you, it flew right out of my head. Thing is, there *is* a room to be had. Mine!"

The expression that Peregrine had interpreted as admiration was in fact skepticism, and astonishment replaced it now. "*Your* room?" Tabby inquired warily.

Mr. Smithton was embarrassed by her suspicions. "Good Gad! I ain't going to be in it. Going back to town with some friends. No point in hanging around, since Vivien didn't show."

Miss Minchin displayed the quickness of wit that Mr. Smithton remembered. "A friend failed to keep an engagement with you?" she asked.

Peregrine was indignant. "I'd hardly suggest you take the room if Vivien was going to be here, would I? Even if he was to be in the neighborhood. 'Twas he who hired

12

it, you see. Had some notion of making a sporting cove out of me. A fellow don't like to tell his friends that they have windmills in their heads, so here I am. Though Vivien may be a bosom bow of mine, for *you* to rub shoulders with him—take my word for it, Miss Minchin, it wouldn't be the thing!''

Tabby was amused by the vehemence of her companion's reply. ''Is he very wicked, your friend?''

Peregrine recognized that note of interest invariably aroused by his friend Vivien in members of the fairer sex. Damned if Perry knew how Viv did it. Despite Perry's own lack of inclination in that direction, he couldn't help being a little envious of his friend's success.

But little Miss Minchin wasn't in Vivien's style at all, which was no doubt to her credit, and her curiosity must be nipped in the bud. ''*Very* wicked,'' Mr. Smithton said sternly. ''On the pathway to perdition. Positively preoccupied with sin.''

Miss Minchin wrinkled her nose. ''I don't scruple to tell you I'm glad I shan't have to meet your friend!'' she said frankly. ''He sounds quite dreadful. So you think you might arrange for me to have your room?''

Mr. Smithton thought this was a nacky notion. ''Don't see why not! Viv never showed up, probably because his fancy—er.'' Peregrine was neither quite so want-witted nor so foxed as to discuss his friend's penchant for fancy pieces with a young lady of gentle birth. ''Er! So I don't see why you shouldn't have it, since I'm leaving and Vivien ain't here. Eh?''

Miss Minchin saw any number of reasons why she shouldn't stay, unchaperoned, in an inn filled to the rafters with sporting gentlemen, in a room bespoke by a rakehell. She also saw that she had little choice. It wouldn't debauch her to spend one night here, surely. On the morrow she would resume her journey to Brighton, and no one would be the wiser. ''What a splendid idea, Perry! I wish your friend no ill, of course, but how glad I am that he failed to meet you here!''

Mr. Smithton was glad also; it warmed his heart to be able to do old Tolly's niece a good turn. Particularly since Miss Minchin was probably the only female in England who failed to appreciate Vivien. It was all that education, Perry decided. Miss Minchin had been too busy with Greek and Hebrew and moral philosophy to develop the usual female addiction to romance. He liked her all the better for it. A pity she wouldn't meet Vivien. Peregrine would have given several ponies he didn't have to see Vivien given a set-down.

He patted Miss Minchin's hand. ''You wait here! I'll fix it up all right and tight!'' he said, and went in search of the innkeeper. Within a short space of time, Tabby was in possession of lodging for the night.

Tabby gazed despondently around the small room; at the narrow little bed, the chair, the small chest of drawers, the water pitcher and bowl on the corner stand. Then she collapsed with relief on the hard bed. There she remained for an unconscionably long time, suffering the full force of the anguish of her separation from her home. Tabby missed her uncle very much. She wished she could share with him her impressions of the journey. She wondered if she would ever meet anyone who understood so well her sense of the absurd.

But she was very weary, and one didn't die of the dumps, after all. Tabby rose from her cramped position and subjected her surroundings to a cursory inspection to ensure she wasn't sharing the chamber with dust-bunnies and assorted insect life. Finding the room neat and clean, she gratefully exchanged her mourning gown for her comfortable old nightdress, blew out the candle, and climbed between the cool rough sheets.

Chapter Three

The hour was far advanced when yet another carriage drew up outside the little inn. Its occupants, too, had suffered the inconvenience of an accident. The driver of this carriage, however, could blame no mischief-making rooster for his mishap. It was his own inattention that had led to the upset—a surprising thing, for Mr. Sanders was a noted whip. But he had been in the midst of a brangle with his current ladybird, and his attention had strayed from the road.

This mortifying fact, the divine Sara—or Sara Divine, as she was known upon the stage—had not let him forget. "At last!" she said now. "What a wretched trip. Once you were very attentive to my comfort, but now—I do not know what I have done to turn you against me, but obviously I have done something, because to drag me out into the country like this is cruel in the greatest degree!"

Mr. Sanders handed his reins to a sleepy groom. "I do not immediately perceive how I have displeased you, my love," he responded with commendable patience. "It was you who wanted to come along."

"You do not understand?" repeated Sara incredulously. "Good God, Vivien! I do not see you for a week, and then you wish me to go into a neighborhood where a prize-fight is being held. As if I should enjoy such a thing!"

Mr. Sanders helped her down from the carriage. "Then you should have said that you didn't care to attend."

"Oh, certainly!" Sara tossed her head. 'Then you would feel perfectly free to go without me, which is probably why you invited me in the first place! You're on the dangle for some other female, I know it! Don't try to pull the wool over *my* eyes!" Those fine dark orbs flashed.

Contrary to the oft-repeated accusations of his current light-o'-love, Mr. Sanders was not particularly interested in any other female. In point of fact, he was not particularly interested in Sara, either. Already today he had endured hysterics and a fainting fit. Now he was expected to coax her once more out of the sullens. Vivien didn't think he cared to do so. Wondering why and how so initially amusing an encounter had turned into so tedious an alliance, he made his way toward the inn.

"Pray do not regard *my* feelings!" gasped Sara, as she trailed after him. "And do not trouble yourself to offer me any word of explanation, because I am very displeased with you." As result of this comment, and innumerable previous comments of a similar nature, it was with considerable energy that Mr. Sanders assaulted the inn door.

That summons was answered by a maidservant, the taproom being long closed and the innkeeper long since asleep beside his cozy wife. The only reason that the maidservant was not snugly tucked up in her own bed was that she was en route to a tryst with one of the grooms. All thought of the groom fled as she surveyed the late-arriving gentleman. His hair was sun-streaked brown, his skin tanned, his shoulders were broad, and his physique muscular; his features were arrogant, and his eyes a startling green. Here was a gentleman, the maidservant thought, who would know instinctively what a lass had on her mind. She reckoned he'd left behind a trail of lasses turned topsy-turvy, not knowing whether they stood on their heads or on their heels. The maidservant dropped an awkward curtsy. "What is it I might be doin' for you, sir?"

Mr. Sanders did indeed recognize the look in the maid-servant's eye, and well he should; the ladies had been running wild for him ever since he'd stepped out of short pants and into the world. It was not a weakness he could appreciate in them. Before he could speak, Sara stepped forward. "Take us to our room, girl!" she commanded in tones as cold as ice.

The maidservant looked, instead, as if she would shut the door in their faces. Mr. Sanders nudged his ladylove aside. "I've a room engaged," he said with a lazy, charming smile that turned the maidservant's knees to jelly on the spot. "And I'd like to avail myself of it, even though the hour is so late."

The maidservant shot a spiteful glance at Sara. "Anything else you might be wishful of, sir? Mayhap something to warm you? 'Tis a chill night."

Sara gasped with outrage at this inference that her luscious person might not generate sufficient warmth to satisfy any man. Vivien smiled again with genuine amusement. "Perhaps some brandy," he suggested diplomatically. Truth be told, he was more than a little tired of this game of hearts that fate seemed determined that he play. He was especially tired of it this evening and watched the maidservant go about his bidding with relief.

Miss Divine also watched the maidservant's departure. Vivien was being very cool toward her. Perhaps she had been a trifle rash. Sara could hardly help it if the suspicion that the charmer of her heart and soul was tiring of her company had turned her into a shrew. She had known when she met him that only a female with more hair than wit would trust Vivien Sanders one inch. Sara had not made that mistake; she did not trust Vivien, but she had made the greater mistake of allowing him a genuine place in her affections. As a result, she was fast in the toils of that green-eyed monster, jealousy. On the one hand, she knew perfectly well that no woman in all of England could compete with her own looks. On the other, she wished to scratch out the eyes of every female who caught Vivien's eye.

Not only ardor roused this determination. On a more practical level—and Sara was very practical—Vivien was a man of substance equal to his looks. "I'm sorry, Vivien!" she whispered. "I know I have been behaving very badly. But 'tis only because of my great regard to you. I know you must forgive me that!"

But Mr. Sanders, at two-and-thirty, was no green lad. This was far from his first venture into romance. Therefore, he was not so quick to reassure Sara as she wished or to succumb again to her caressing ways. "Yes, you have been behaving badly," he said merely, and greeted the maidservant's return with scarcely disguised relief. The wench lighted them up the stairs. In silence, they followed her down the hall.

The maidservant opened a door. Regally, Sara swept past her and into the room. Mr. Sanders murmured an inquiry, received an answer, then also stepped within.

Now was the moment. Sara turned and gazed at Vivien with dark, mournful eyes. Her lower lip was atremble. A perfect tear trickled down her cheek.

She waited. Nothing happened. Vivien watched her with a sardonic air. "Bravo, my love! Tragedy personified. To what end, pray?"

The tear disappeared as if by magic. Sara stamped her dainty foot "Oh! You are the most exasperating wretch!"

Sara *was* a lovely creature, as anyone must attest, ivory-skinned and raven-haired, slender and elegant—and very spoiled. And she was on the verge of flying into the boughs again, as must be evident to anyone who knew the signs.

Vivien knew the signs, none better. "I'll leave you now," he said coolly, and walked toward the door.

Sara ran after him. "Where are you going?" she cried. "Surely not after that slattern—even you would not stoop so low!" She glimpsed his expression then, and knew she'd gone too far. "I didn't mean that, Vivien! You know I did not! I was just so angry—I cannot bear the thought of your so much as glancing at another woman. You will not dislike that in me, I know!"

Sara was mistaken. Vivien very much disliked that in her. He interrupted her apologies. "I'll thank you, madam, to be a little less busy about my affairs." Sara fell back a step, as if he'd struck her, pressed a hand to her heart. Vivien turned away and walked through the door. In the hallway outside he paused and listened. Had he remained in the room, his cruelty—or so she would have termed it—would have caused her to languish about as feebly as if he'd wounded her to the heart. His absence seemed to have a beneficial effect. He could hear her muffled curses through the thickness of the closed door.

Vivien sighed. He was not a cruel man. Nor was he one to be tied to a woman's apron-strings. Not even the apron-stings of so divinely avaricious a creature as Sara. Theirs was a liaison based on a mutual attraction that both had known would soon fade. At least, Vivien had known. Apparently Sara had not. Another curse assaulted his ears. It sounded nearer the door. A tantrum at this moment was more than Vivien could endure. He turned and made his way down the hall to the room the dazzled maidservant had told him was that of his friend Peregrine.

19

Chapter Four

Tabby tossed and turned on the hard mattress. What a day it had been. Fancy encountering Perry again like that. And a good thing it was she had, else Tabby might have spent this night without a roof over her head. How her uncle would have laughed to see his pupil turned into a man-milliner. Tabby smiled.

It was then she heard the door open and footsteps enter the room. For one horrid moment, Tabby wondered if Perry had thought up some dastardly plot against her virtue. Then she realized the absurdity of that notion. Still, the fact remained that there was an intruder in her bedchamber. Tabby thought of all the sporting gentlemen who had frequented the inn this day. Judging from the sounds that had issued from the building, several of those gentlemen had been, if not as drunk as an emperor, at least as drunk as a lord. And now one of those same gentlemen had invaded her bedchamber. Tabby couldn't think what to do. She drew herself up into as small a space as possible on the far side of the bed.

The footsteps paused. Tabby heard a muttered curse, saw a flare of light. Some strange intruder this, who lit a candle to go about his nefarious business. Tabby scrunched down farther beneath the covers, wishing she'd had the foresight to pull them up over her head. She heard movement, and then nothing. Tabby couldn't bear the suspense. Very cautiously, she opened her eyes and looked out into the room.

A very handsome green-eyed gentleman was seated in the room's one chair. As Tabby watched, he raised a brandy snifter to his lips. Tabby thought he seemed to be listening. Apparently satisfied with what he heard, or failed to hear, he then shrugged out of his well-fitting jacket, cravat, and linen shirt before Tabby's horrified eyes. She should protest, she knew. But what on earth was she to say? The gentleman was obviously in his altitudes. He bent to draw off his boots. Tabby closed her eyes and prayed.

Due to the effects of brandy on an empty stomach, Mr. Sanders was not entirely sober, though not so far into his cups as Tabby thought. For his condition he must not be censured, for he had endured the devil of a day, and this was a hard-drinking age. Speculating upon how smuggled French brandy, for such it surely was, might have come into the possession of the owner of the inn, he bent to address his boots.

It was not a prudent posture. Vivien's head swam. Moreover, he was hallucinating that he was staring at a battered portmanteau. Vivien knew perfectly well that his friend Perry would never own such a shabby article. Slowly, he straightened, picked up the candle, surveyed the small room. His bewildered gaze fell upon a drab gown hung carefully from a hook on the wall, and other items of unmistakably feminine apparel. Where the deuce was Perry? Vivien stepped closer to the bed. At first he thought it empty. Then he glimpsed a tangle of brown curls.

Mr. Sanders surveyed those rumpled curls. His expression was incredulous. Whoever would have thought that Perry—? The sly dog! But Vivien could hardly spend the night in the same chamber as his friend's peculiar. He would have to wake her to discover Perry's whereabouts.

Gingerly, Vivien reached out and touched the bedclothes in the vicinity of what must be the damsel's shoulder, or so he adjudged by the position of her curly head. "Pray pardon me, miss," he murmured, "but I must—ouch!" The sentence was broke off when she abruptly darted out from beneath the bedclothes and her elbow collided painfully with his nose.

Vivien tenderly inspected that injured article before he grabbed for his assailant. She eluded him. Naturally, Vivien went after her. In this manner, they passed a couple of times around the small room. Then Tabby made the tactical error of moving into the corner where the washstand and basin stood. Vivien caught her by the arms. What he should have done at that moment was explain to Miss Minchin that he hadn't the slightest design upon her virtue, of course. But the thrill of the chase was upon him, and the effects of the brandy had not yet worn off. Furthermore, Tabby did look quite fetching, with her gray eyes open wide and her brown curls cascading over her shoulders and her plump bosom heaving as she gasped for breath.

To all this provocation, Mr. Sanders responded as any rakehell must. He bent his head and kissed his captive thoroughly. And to this embrace, Tabby responded also as befitted her upbringing and character. She reached behind her and grasped the water pitcher and emptied it over Vivien's head. He released her, cursing. Tabby darted across the room.

"I know who you are!" she said indignantly, from what she fancied was a safe position behind the chair. "The rakehell! Perry warned me about you. And *I* warn you that I shall scream loud enough to wake the dead if you lay another hand on me, sir!"

Vivien had no desire to lay hands on this little spitfire,

who he feared had done permanent damage to both his jacket and his nose, not to mention his pride. He wiped the water from his face and eyed his assailant with some bewilderment. This was a queer kettle of fish altogether. Though Vivien had not known quite so many high-flyers as Perry attributed to him during the course of his career, he had known enough to think this damsel's shabby night-dress an odd garment for a romantic rendezvous. For that matter, Perry was an odd person to rendezvous with. "*If* you scream loud enough to wake the dead, you'll also wake everyone else in this benighted place," Vivien pointed out. "And I don't think you want that."

This suggestion gave Tabby pause. A lady's reputation resided not in what she did, but in what she might be considered to have done. What Tabby might be considered to have done whilst closeted with a rakehell would hardly qualify her to serve as governess to the daughters of a baronet. "Very well, then, I shan't scream!" she said hastily. "But you would oblige me if you would leave this room at once, sir!"

The reprehensible Mr. Sanders, however, was beginning to enjoy himself. It wasn't often that he found himself alone with a female who regarded him with such obvious disapproval. She was a taking little thing, he thought, this plump little person with her tousled brown curls and cen-sorious gray eyes. Not in his style, of course, nor would he have thought her in Perry's. "What *have* you done with Perry?" he asked.

"What have I done with Perry?" she echoed blankly. Then her cheeks flamed. "Oh! You think that I—that Perry—" She broke off and buried her cheeks in her hands. Vivien sighed and steeled himself to deal with yet another hysterical female. Then she raised her head and he saw that she was laughing. "How absurd!" she gasped.

Vivien could not help but enjoy her laughter. He'd heard precious little female merriment of late. "I begin to think

23

the both of us are laboring under awkward misapprehensions," he remarked as he sat down on the bed. "That you are not a lady of equivocal occupation, as I am not a wicked reprobate."

There seemed a safe distance between them. Tabby perched warily on the edge of the chair. "Well, I know I'm not a prime article of virtue," she said, then blushed again. "That is to say, I *am* a respectable female! But as for you, Perry did say that you are on the downward road to perdition, sir!"

"Ah." Vivien leaned back on the pillow. "And I've given you no reason to think otherwise, having assaulted you, after all. Accept my sincere apologies for that, Miss—"

Tabby wasn't about to make this winsome reprobate acquainted with her name. "Never mind," she said.

"Miss Nevermind." He smiled. "I promise you that I am in no mood for a bit of frolic—and you have made it abundantly clear that neither are you!" She looked skeptical, and he quirked a brow. "I am not half so black as I am painted, truly. It's all the fault of my accursed face and the wagging tongues of my friends. They provide me with a name, and I must live up to it, lest I suffer their disappointment. In truth, I'm as innocent as a babe newborn."

Tabby recalled the knowing way in which the babe newborn had kissed her. "What a clanker! Although I should not say so, I suppose."

"Of course you should," said Mr. Sanders, with a note of laughter in his voice that plucked at Tabby's heart. If his reputation was overstated, she thought ruefully, it was not wholly undeserved. He added humorously, "I think we may be said to have bypassed the usual formalities. There, I have made you smile. You forgive me, then. But you have not yet told me how it comes about that you are here and Perry is not."

Tabby sensed instinctively that the less this gentleman

24

knew of her the better. She was finding it damnably difficult to gaze anywhere but at his naked chest. "Perry went back to town with his friends. That left his room vacant, and I was in need of one, and so he gave it to me."

Mr. Sanders found it difficult to credit his friend with so chivalrous an act. "Now you *have* piqued my interest," he said. "But never fear, Miss Nevermind, I shan't pry into your secrets. Any friend of Perry's—and so you must be!—must also be a friend of mine." So saying, he rose. Tabby rose also and with alacrity ducked behind the chair.

Vivien laughed to see her in that posture, clutching at the chair as if she were a tamer of wild beasts and he a lion. Here was one female whose high admiration he obviously did not excite. "You're safe with me, Miss Nevermind," he said, as he picked up his shirt from the floor where he'd previously let it fall. "I give you my word that I shan't make a violent attack on your virtue."

Of course he would not, Tabby realized. Why should so very fine a gentleman cherish ambitions upon her own small and plump and insignificant person, when the large majority of high-flyers in the kingdom must be fighting tooth and nail to cast themselves at his feet? Silly widgeons! "How very foolish you must think me," Tabby said, shyly. "And I owe you an apology, I think. It must be deuced inconvenient—I mean, it must not be wholly pleasant to be in possession of a reputation such as yours, sir! You are making a dreadful muddle of those shirt buttons. Let me help you, pray."

Vivien was not averse to some assistance. Tabby crossed the room and applied herself to the task of buttoning the rakehell's shirt and thus sparing herself further sight of his bronzed bare chest. Her fingers were not quite steady. No one had ever kissed her before. Or wandered about in her presence in a state of undress.

Tabby was feeling very sad. On the morrow she was off

to Brighton to a life of hired servitude, after all. She glanced up with innocent longing into Vivien's wicked face. Vivien was oddly moved by that glance. He gripped her shoulders.

At that most inopportune of moments, the door flew open. The divine Sara stood on the threshold, in a state of quite fetching *déshabillé*. "Well!" she cried in heartfelt tones, as one glance at the guilty-looking couple fulfilled her direct fantasies. Clutching dramatically at her breast, she staggered forward. "Wretch! Heartless beast! Seducer!" And then she swooned gracefully to the floor.

Chapter Five

Miss Ermyntrude Elphinstone stood gazing out the window of her papa's rather charming house on Brighton's Marine Parade, which stretched for a considerable extent along the sea. The view was quite delightful, of blue skies and windswept trees and waves pounding on the soft white cliffs. The view also afforded a clear view of anyone approaching Sir Geoffrey's house, and it was this latter circumstance that accounted for the gloomy expression on Ermy's pretty face. She glimpsed a shabby coach. It did not interest her especially; only the carriage of a certain viscount could do that. Idly, Ermyntrude decided the shabby vehicle must have lost its way. She was surprised to see it stop in front of the house. Perhaps St. Erth had suffered an accident to his own carriage? Perhaps it suited him to travel about in this queer vehicle, incognito, so to speak? Ermyntrude didn't care if the viscount came calling in a dogcart, just so long as he appeared. She leaned forward in the window, the better to see. No elegant golden-haired lordling descended from the coach, however, merely one drab-looking female carrying a very shabby portmanteau.

The female turned toward the house. ''Drusilla!'' said Ermyntrude over her shoulder to her sister, who was putting together a map of Europe with the assistance of her inseparable companion, a large, multicolored, and very shaggy hound of indeterminate ancestry known as Lambchop. "That female that Pa hired—I think she's here."

"Oh, fudge!" retorted Drusilla rudely. "I was hoping she'd had a better offer. Or been kidnapped, or worse!"

Ermyntrude couldn't argue with this sentiment. It was one thing to hire a tutor for Drusilla, who was still in the schoolroom; but at seventeen, Ermyntrude already knew more than she wished about geography and history and other matters of a similarly dull nature. Why her father had hired this female, Ermyntrude wasn't certain. She suspected, from his evasiveness when she'd broached the subject, that Sir Geoffrey was none too certain himself. "Where *is* Pa?" she asked.

"Don't know." Drusilla was preoccupied with trying to decide where Asia Minor fit into her map. "I think he went out."

"I suppose we'd better let her in." Ermyntrude sighed and wandered out into the hall.

It was an elegantly furnished hallway—as was, indeed, the rest of Sir Geoffrey's house. The walls of the drawing room, for example, were japanned in soft shades of slate and green, with gilt decoration; the sides of the ceiling were coved; and Brussels carpeting in a trailing floral pattern on a cream ground covered the floor. Ermyntrude paused by a circular convex mirror hung in the hallway and studied herself. Her features, she decided, were perfect enough to grace a cameo, her hair was a lovely shade of red-gold, and her eyes as blue as the sky outside the window through which she had recently stared. How flattering this new gown was, fashioned of clinging white muslin, with a plain, brief bodice and a narrow skirt that fell straight and close to the figure from its high waistline. A pity St. Erth was not about to see her looking so fine. What accounted for this omission? Why could not the viscount appreciate just how very near perfection Ermyntrude was? How could such a paragon be so deficient in good taste? Ermyntrude twisted a curl thoughtfully around her finger. Perhaps he would prove more attentive if she tried a new hairstyle.

Consequently, it was Drusilla who opened the door, the problem of Asia Minor having been solved by Lambchop, who had decided that the puzzle piece upon which his mistress lavished such attention could only be a tasty morsel for him to eat. "You'd better come in," Drusilla said ungraciously. "You could've come in sooner, but Ermy fell to studying her postures before the looking glass."

"I did no such thing!" protested Ermyntrude, as she hastily stepped away from the mirror and joined her sister at the door. Frankly, she inspected their visitor. Crushed bonnet, battered portmanteau—and then her gaze moved to Tabby's face. "Good gracious!" said Ermyntrude. "We thought you'd be quite old."

Drusilla, too, inspected Tabby. "Yes," she said frankly. "And prune faced. You ain't either. For my part, I'm just as glad. If I must be told how to be a lady, at least it won't be by someone with an ugly phiz."

Teach this hoyden to be a lady? Tabby wondered if she was equal to the task. For her part, she had expected her charges to be considerably younger. She had also not expected to be met by them at the doorway. "This *is* the household of Sir Geoffrey Elphinstone?" she asked.

"She's as surprised as we are," observed Drusilla to her sister. Ermyntrude's attention had again wandered— she was craning her neck for a glimpse of a more elegant carriage—but Lambchop waved his great plumed tail. Drusilla pushed him out of the way. "Come in," she said again. "We don't know where he's got to, but Pa's around somewhere. He had the notion you was supposed to be here yesterday, but I suppose it was a mistake."

Tabby suspected that there had indeed been some mis-

29

take made, on her part. She was forming a very unusual picture of life in the Elphinstone household. Indeed, she was suffering an attack of craven-heartedness so severe that, had not Drusilla taken away her portmanteau, she might have turned tail and fled. But she had nowhere to go, Tabby reminded herself. Perhaps she was merely shaken from the carriage ride—the job-coachman had attempted to make up for the delay by driving the remainder of the journey as if the hounds of hell were in hot pursuit—and matters in this household were not in so bad a case as they seemed. And perhaps Tabby was whistling in the dark, as she followed Drusilla and Lambchop and her portmanteau down the hallway and into the drawing room.

Ermyntrude trailed after them. "I'm hungry," she said plaintively. "We should have some tea. I'll just go and fetch it, shall I?"

"No!" Drusilla set down the portmanteau. "If you go fetch it, we'll see neither you nor the tea for upward of an hour. I'll go. You stay here and keep Miss company."

The younger of Tabby's charges, at least, possessed a lively intelligence, Tabby decided, even if her manners were appalling. "Why not have one of the servants fetch the tea?" she asked, not unreasonably.

"The servants?" scoffed Drusilla. "If we left the servants to do it, we'd wait longer than an hour. I'll be right back! Ermy will entertain you, miss!" She left the room with Lambchop at her heels.

Tabby gazed around the drawing room. Tables, couches, and sofas were studiously disarranged around the classical marble fireplace as if the family had just left them—or as if the room had not had attention from the servants for some time. But the furnishings were of good quality, of mahogany and rosewood inlaid with brass. Ermyntrude sank down on the circular ottoman and gazed out the window. Tabby perched on a parlor chair of boldly striped brown-and-white zebrawood.

The silence threatened to become oppressive. "Pardon me," said Tabby. "I *have* come to the right house?"

Ermyntrude turned reluctantly from the window. "And Pa calls me skitter-witted!" She laughed. "You were wishful of a place, and Pa heard about it and took it into his head that you'd do fine for us, though heaven knows why! No offense, miss. But I think if I was you, I'd rather be a poor relation than hire myself out to someone else's family."

So would Tabby, had she a choice; but she had lost her mama early—the lady had grown exasperated by a spouse who was neither comfortably endowed nor of particularly ambitious temperament, and had left him to pursue his humdrum existence while she set out to explore the larger world. Tabby's papa had fallen victim shortly thereafter to a riding accident. Now, with the death of her only remaining relative, Tabby had nowhere else to turn. As a result of innate curiosity and an indulgent uncle, she had received an education far beyond that usually allowed her sex; but most prospective employers would have taken a dim view of her youth and her total lack of practical experience. "I am fortunate to have found this position," Tabby said.

"I suppose," Ermyntrude said doubtfully. Gratitude was not an emotion with which she had much experience. "For myself, I'd rather marry. Indeed, I shall marry! Probably before I am eighteen."

Tabby, too, had once assumed she'd marry, perhaps some student of her uncle's who shared her ability to laugh at the world. Now that seemed unlikely. As an employee in Sir Geoffrey's household, Tabby would be neither fish nor fowl. A curious sense of anticlimax gripped her. It was one thing to be offered a position by a stranger and quite another to face the reality of the thing. Tabby had no clear notion even of what Sir Geoffrey wished her duties to be. His man of business had been very vague. Tabby had assumed that the daughters of the house would benefit from English and French grammar, writing, arithmetic and music, geography and the globes. She had prepared for her new situation in life as best she could, with Miss Mangall's *Historical and Miscellaneous Questions for the Use of Young People* tucked away in her shabby portmanteau. Now, even with this excellent volume at her disposal, Tabby was feeling very inadequate. Would she be given her own room? Or housed with the other servants in some stifling nook beneath the eaves?

Drusilla walked into the room then, balancing a tea tray. Tabby accepted a teacup and tried to take encouragement from the map of Europe laid out on the floor. The fact that Asia Minor was missing altogether seemed ominous, alas. Tabby told herself that she was merely tired and therefore seeing only the gloomy side of things. She'd feel better after a good night's sleep uninterrupted by rakehells and their *petite amies*, and roosters crowing outside her window—perhaps in hope of another buttered muffin—at the crack of dawn.

She returned to the present and found Drusilla watching her. How odd that it should be left to a child to do the honors of the house. "Is your mama also not at home?" Tabby inquired. It was a somewhat presumptuous question for a hireling, but Tabby was feeling a trifle desperate.

"Ma?" Drusilla echoed indistinctly, her mouth of tea biscuit. So shocked did she appear that Tabby wondered briefly if the girl's mother had also run off. This notion that a bond might exist between them was shattered by Ermyntrude's laughter. "We don't have a ma!" she said. "We did, of course—and that we do no longer is entirely Dru's fault!"

Drusilla's fault? The child shot a venomous glance at her sister, inspiring Tabby with a grisly vision of violent deeds enacted in Elphinstone House. "Ma died in childbed," Drusilla said to Tabby. "After giving birth to me. Ermy likes to make out I killed her, which I didn't, and it's hardly fair of her to take on so about it since I'd as soon have a ma as not!''

"You will!'' Ermyntrude said spitefully. "Lady Grey!''

This comment for some reason plunged both the girls into gloom. Tabby almost sighed aloud, so relieved was she to discover that she was not expected to impart the niceties of polite behavior to a youthful murderess.

But just what *was* she to impart? Ermyntrude's last remark had suggested that Sir Geoffrey planned to rewed soon. Surely his new wife would wish to oversee the education of his daughters? They were hardly of an age to require either a companion or a governess. Ermyntrude must surely soon make her come-out, and Drusilla was not so many years younger. These confusing speculations were giving Tabby a headache. She reached for another tea biscuit, only to discover that Lambchop had taken advantage of his mistress's inattention to make a clean sweep with his large tongue of all the tea biscuits on the plate; though the dog was named after its favorite food, any adequate substitute would do. Drusilla became belatedly aware of her pet's depredations. "Lambchop! Look what you've done! Now there'll be nothing more to eat till dinner, and heaven knows when *that*'ll be!''

The hound withdrew to the ottoman, flopped down despondently. Tabby was rendered equally unhappy by Drusilla's ominous remark about dinner; she had not eaten since some time the day before.

Drusilla's next comment was even more ominous. "*You*'ll know what to do about that, miss!'' she said. "Pa hired you in the very nick of time! Cook has a fondness for the cooking sherry, you see, and the butler for the maids, and the housekeeper gave notice a month ago saying such conditions wasn't what she was used to or could like!''

Tabby's heart sank. She knew that some employers expected a governess not only to take complete charge of her pupils but also to undertake the housekeeping and perhaps even some sewing, until all her waking hours were filled. At least Tabby might be grateful that sewing had thus far not been mentioned; she was not very good at needlework. She must be grateful also for the handsome wage that was being paid her, a full twenty-five guineas a year, which she had vowed to save until she might open her own school. It was not the future that she had envisioned for herself, perhaps, but still a prospect far rosier than any she'd imagined before Sir Geoffrey's man of business had contacted her in response to her somewhat daring newspaper advertisement.

"You're mighty quiet, miss!" observed Drusilla. "Perhaps you've decided we won't suit." Before Tabby could demur, Lambchop jumped down from the ottoman and rushed, barking, through the door. "Pa," added Drusilla, in explanation of the footsteps that sounded in the hall. "Ermy, don't sit on that ottoman, or you'll get Lambchop's hair all over your pretty dress."

Ermyntrude looked down at the pretty dress, which, apparently, no handsome young viscount would have the opportunity to admire this day. "It doesn't signify." She sighed and reclaimed her window seat.

Drusilla grimaced at her sister's back, then turned to Tabby. "I hope you ain't taken us in dislike! Although it wouldn't surprise me if you had. Lady Grey considers us a bit of an oddity, and I suppose she's right, and I suppose we must try to mend our ways, for Pa's sake. I think I should tell you that Pa has pinned his hopes on you. And so have we all! *Not* that I need a governess, you understand! We've tried to rub along by ourselves, but Pa hasn't the faintest notion of how to go on, and I'm too young, and Ermy—well, Ermy is what she is!" She shot her sister an unappreciative glance. "Perhaps I shan't grow up. I

34

don't want to grow up if it means that I must go about acting like I have windmills in my head.''

"Windmills!" In her indignation, Ermyntrude sat up straight. "Just wait! Because you *will* grow up, and you'll grow up into a beauty just like I did, and *then* we'll see!"

"I *shan't* be a beauty!" retorted Drusilla with determination, although her looks already made a mockery of her words. "And if I *am*, I promise that I won't go about so full of my amours that I can talk of nothing else, and generally make such a cake of myself that everyone around me either wants to wring my neck or fall into whoops!"

The younger Elphinstone was certainly outspoken. And it was obvious from Ermyntrude's expression that this plainspokenness had caught her on the raw. "Pray don't do violence to your feelings!" Tabby said hastily, because Ermyntrude looked ready to fly into the boughs. Lambchop's barks and the footsteps drew closer. A gentleman walked into the drawing room. Tabby knew immediately from his resemblance to his daughters that it must be Sir Geoffrey. He was an extraordinarily handsome man.

Apparently Sir Geoffrey found nothing untoward in the fact that his daughters were glaring daggers at each other. "Down, beast! Not you, Miss Minchin," he added, for Tabby had risen on his entrance. "You *are* Miss Minchin? Good! I am pleased to make your acquaintance, ma'am. You have been having a pleasant little coze with my girls, have you? Good! We wish you to feel quite at home here with us, for we are all very grateful to you for having come to take us in hand!''

Chapter Six

Life in the Elphinstone household was every bit as eccentric as Tabby had feared. Like the rickety job-coach Sir Geoffrey had hired to bring her to Brighton, the household had a ramshackle air. In point of fact, matters were at so bad a pass that Tabby found herself compelled to enlighten the housemaids about, among other things, the introduction of tea leaves to the carpet and damp sand to the floor, with the result that she had little time to spend with the young ladies of the house. Still, though she had not the time she'd like to spend upon either endeavor, some progress had been made. Sir Geoffrey had commented only yesterday upon the fact that, for two days running, breakfast had been on the table at a conventional hour. And as for Tabby's charges, perhaps she had had little opportunity to instruct them in such weighty matters as moral philosophy, but Drusilla had begun to sit more often on the furniture than the floor, and Lambchop was less frequently seen in the dining room at mealtimes, and Ermyntrude had been heard to inform a footman that the proper way to crack the claws of a lobster at dinner was in the kitchen and not between the hinges of a dining room drawer. All in all, thought Tabby, she was growing very comfortable with the Elphinstones. Although, perhaps, considering the oddities of the family, that wasn't an altogether good thing. Tabby wondered what her uncle would have made of Sir Geoffrey and his offspring, and smiled.

Ermyntrude saw that smile, interpreted it is an indication of Tabby's pleasure at being at the theater. "I said you would enjoy it!" she whispered now. "As for your being in mourning, nobody knows you, so what can it signify? Myself, I've never understood how it befitted the dead if the living made themselves miserable! Yes, and each other also. Look at Pa!"

Sir Geoffrey was in mourning? Confused, Tabby glanced at her employer, seated in the front of the hired box. Far from looking stricken, he gave every indication of a gentleman hugely enjoying himself. "I don't understand," Tabby said.

"Clunch!" said Ermyntrude fondly. "Oh, I forgot that you haven't met Lady Grey. She was to join us tonight, but came down with one of her sick headaches. *She* is in mourning also, but it hasn't stopped her from leading Pa a merry dance, despite the fact that she's supposed to be in Brighton because of health. Yes, and the deuced female means to put our nerves in as sad a state as hers are supposed to be, or I don't know chalk from cheese! Well, I shan't let her. Oh, look! There is St. Erth."

Tabby was reminded of her responsibilities. "I don't think your papa would care to hear you refer to his future wife as 'deuced,' " she said.

"Fiddlestick!" retorted Ermyntrude. "I've heard him call her that himself. Yes, and I've heard you say worse! So for you to scold me is like the pot calling the kettle black. But you are missing St. Erth!"

Tabby had already heard far more of the viscount than she cared to. Ermyntrude's constant effusions had inspired her with an acute dislike of the young gentleman. Cravenly, she avoided glancing at the opposite box. It had been some time since Tabby had been to a play, and despite her reservations, she could not help but enjoy the treat. The

37

theater was crowded, box and galley and pit, with gentle-folk and their servants, tradesmen and cits, and military men. Tabby inhaled that extraordinary compound of odd scents peculiar to a theater, of which lamp oil and stale bodies made up no small part.

"There!" hissed Ermyntrude, and nudged her once again. "Do pay attention, Tabby! Isn't St. Erth the most splendid-looking gentleman you have ever laid eyes upon?"

Tabby murmured noncommittally. In truth, she could not see clearly enough to judge more than that St. Erth was tall and apparently well built, with golden hair, and attention fixed firmly on the stage. Tabby would have liked similarly to direct her own attention thither, at a subterranean vault set up complete with coffins, death's-heads and crossbows, toads and snails. But it was not the scenery that had caught the viscount's attention, she realized. Tabby also stared at the slender, raven-haired actress who dominated the stage. From so great a distance, Tabby could not see the color of the lady's eyes, but she would recognize that histrionic manner anywhere. The actress placed a hand to her breast. Tabby shuddered and sank back in her chair.

Ermyntrude, too, noticed the viscount's keen interest. "It isn't true that St. Erth is on the dangle for that female!" she announced, so shrilly that her papa glanced back at her and frowned. "It is just that she is all the rage right now, and so he follows the example set by his friends. The divine Sara, they call her. I'll wager she's not so divine seen at close range. She's probably thirty if she's a day!"

As Tabby remembered, the divine Sara had not looked particularly haggish at closer view. Quite the opposite. And her vocabulary had been awesome, when she recovered from her swoon. Naturally, Tabby could not apprise Ermyntrude of her acquaintance with the actress.

Much as Ermyntrude might enjoy the story, she could not be trusted to keep it to herself, and any employer must consider it an excellent reason to turn Tabby off. Tabby leaned back farther into the shadows, wishing she had the knack of making herself invisible.

The play was quite ruined for her. Tabby was unable even to appreciate Rogero's long soliloquy and his announcement that "Despair sits brooding over the putrid eggs of hope." The glimpse of Sara had quite naturally reminded her of a certain rakehell and her own shocking behavior so far as he was concerned. She was a fine one to chide Ermyntrude, she thought; she who had emptied a water pitcher over a gentleman, and then kissed him and buttoned his shirt. If anyone were ever to find out—

"Miss Minchin." Tabby started to hear her name. So deep had she been in her brown study that she had failed to notice that the soliloquy had concluded with guitar and a song, the winds had ceased to whistle through the caverns with the arrival of an intermission, and that several people had come to Sir Geoffrey's box. One of the gentlemen had spoken to her and was smiling at her now. Behind him, Ermyntrude grimaced meaningfully. "Gracious, but you are one for air-dreaming, Tabby!" she said. "I was wishful of making you acquainted with Mr. Philpotts."

Ermyntrude did not want for admirers, though St. Erth was not among them. Tabby murmured a polite greeting. Mr. Philpotts was no Adonis, perhaps, but there was a twinkle in his brown eyes and his expression was kind. "Welcome to Brighton, Miss Minchin," he said. "Ermy speaks highly of you. How fortunate it was that Sir Geoffrey found you—a boon for all concerned."

"Ermy," was it? This was no small degree of familiarity to accord to a gentleman. Tabby glanced around for her wayward charge, saw Ermyntrude wriggle her fingers in an attempt to catch the attention of St. Erth. She succeeded. The viscount looked rather astonished at the familiarity, whereas Mr. Philpotts looked bleak. It was clearly midsummer moon with the poor gentleman. Tabby was tempted to suggest he might go on more prosperously if he didn't wear his heart upon his sleeve.

Ermyntrude turned away, her expression sulky. Tabby held her breath, anticipating a storm. "May I," Mr. Philpotts interjected smoothly, "fetch you ladies some lemonade?"

"What a splendid notion!" Ermyntrude was all smiles. "I'll just come with you, shall I?" She caught his arm and led him out into the hall.

Ermyntrude's exit distracted Sir Geoffrey from the conversation he was having with a couple of his cronies. Lady Grey wouldn't like it if Ermy made a cake of herself at the theater, he realized. Nor would she like it if he appeared to be enjoying Miss Minchin's company. "Better go along!" he advised Tabby. "Appearances, you know!"

Glumly, Tabby rose. She would much rather have remained quiet as a little mouse in a dark corner of the box. But Sir Geoffrey was her employer, and his wish was her command.

She stepped through the door and out into the hall, where various other playgoers visited and strolled. Nowhere did she glimpse Ermyntrude and Mr. Philpotts. Tabby had no notion of where one went to procure lemonade in a theater, and she disliked to draw attention to herself by stopping someone to ask. Helplessly, she moved with the flow of traffic. At least, she told herself, she was unlikely to encounter the divine Sara in this crush. She was apparently little more likely to encounter Osbert and Ermy. Tabby was soon quite lost. She turned down this corridor and that, and then found herself backstage.

There were fewer people here, if further obstacles in the form of trailing ropes and miscellaneous pieces of scenery. Tabby paused to contemplate clouds painted in semitransparent colors on linen stretched on frames. A hand caught her arm. Startled, Tabby glanced up into bright green eyes and a wickedly handsome face. She supposed she should not have been surprised. Where the divine Sara went, Vivien would not be far behind.

Vivien, however, had not the advantage of Tabby's forewarning, and he was startled, indeed. "It *is* you!" he said. "I thought for a moment I was seeing a ghost—or a figment of my imagination come to life! I make you my compliments, Miss Nevermind. You look surprised. Can it be you have forgotten me so soon?"

Forget the gentleman who had bestowed upon her her first kiss, and additionally her first glimpse of a bronzed naked chest? Tabby suspected she would remember the wicked Vivien even on her deathbed. But she was here to prevent Ermyntrude making à cake of herself over a gentleman, not to make one of herself. "Why should I remember you, pray?"

So she wished to play games with him? Vivien quirked a brow. "So many gentlemen have made violent attacks on your virtue recently that I am lost among the crowd?"

Tabby couldn't repress her ready sense of humor. "It is your memory that is at fault. I am the female whose virtue you promised was quite safe!"

"Did I?" Vivien smiled. "I must have been foxed. I am glad to have this opportunity to offer you my apologies."

How very fine he was, in frilled shirt and knee breeches and long-tailed coat. Tabby was aware of how drab she must look in her dreary dark gown. And then she wondered at herself, for she had never thought much about her appearance. "Nothing of the sort!" she said briskly, in a last-ditch effort to withstand her captor's devastating charm. "You refer to the, er, climax of our last meeting, I suppose. It doesn't signify."

"Oh?" Vivien guided Tabby farther away from the backstage bustle, between two of a series of shutters or flats that opened centrally and moved in grooves set in and about the stage. "You enjoyed being called a doxy, a trollop, Haymarket-ware? If that is what you like, I shall be happy to oblige you—little jade!"

Tabby remembered all too clearly how Sara, recovering from her swoon, had denounced Vivien for carrying on a squalid little intrigue behind her back. How embarrassed Tabby had been. And how lightly Vivien seemed to regard the episode. Her amusement faded. "You are outrageous, sir!" she said.

"I try to be," Vivien admitted. "There is my reputation to live up to, you will recall. What a surprise to encounter you like this. When I made inquiries the next day, you had already left the inn. No one seemed to know where you had come from or who you were. Now here you are. Fortune has smiled on me."

Tabby refused to be disarmed. "*Very* outrageous!" she said. "It is no wonder you have a wicked reputation, sir, if this is how you talk to all chance-met females!"

Vivien threw back his head and laughed aloud. "Not all, I assure you; only those who amuse me. You are not in the ordinary way, are you, Miss Nevermind?"

"I am not a goose-cap, if that is what you mean," Tabby responded dryly. "You are amusing yourself by throwing the hatchet at me, I think. And in that case, you have only yourself to blame if people are bird-witted enough to take you seriously."

Had he just been delivered yet another set-down? "Unjust! You do amuse me; I have just said so." Vivien dropped his bantering attitude. "I think perhaps that I should call you 'witch.' I have not been able to put you out of my mind."

Perry had not exaggerated; his friend was very wicked and very dangerous, indeed. Tabby forced her thoughts away from kisses and naked chests. A liaison with the divine Sara was one thing; everyone reared outside a convent knew about gentlemen and their ladybirds. But Tabby was very disappointed to realize that Vivien would try to trifle with even a plump little nobody like herself.

Vivien was watching her, trying to read the expressions that flitted across her face—and Vivien's opinion of that face was much kinder than Tabby's own. He thought her not a great beauty, perhaps, but considerably more appealing than several great beauties he knew, one of whom was even at this moment waiting in the green room for him to pay her homage and make up to her for their latest quarrel, which had been occasioned by his frowning on her in bed.

Let Sara wait. "Black doesn't suit you," he said. "I'd like to see you in light green or blue."

This remark put Tabby in mind of the manner in which she would like to see Vivien, wicked rakehell or no. The nature of that reflection led her to the unsettling conclusion that she was as depraved as he. Clearly it was foolish to prolong this conversation. "I must go," she murmured. "My, er, friends will be wondering what has become of me."

"Wait." Vivien caught her hand. "Have I offended you? I did not mean to."

Tabby felt the warmth of his hand, even through her glove. She remembered the touch of her own fingers against his bare chest. Scant wonder that the man spoke so freely to her, Tabby thought, and flushed as she remembered how she had practically invited him to repeat his kiss. "No!" she gasped, and sought to free herself.

Vivien frowned and released her. "Surely you can't be afraid of me!" he said.

"No! Yes!" Tabby could hardly explain that what she feared was her immense longing to hurl herself on the wicked rakehell's chest. "I must go!" she said again, and ducked around the flats. This time it was with a deliberate effort that she lost herself in the crowd, wandering aimlessly for a time until she succeeded in pushing Vivien to the back of her mind. Only then did she make her way back to Sir Geoffrey's box. What would her employer say when she returned without Ermyntrude and Mr. Philpotts? Perhaps he would ring a peal over her. Tabby almost wished for this, as if it would relieve her conflicted feelings somewhat to be read a dreadful scold.

But Sir Geoffrey at that moment had conflicted feelings of his own. Tabby entered the box to find him staring at a blond woman who'd entered St. Erth's box. She raised her hand and waved.

Sir Geoffrey did not return the salute. His expression was remarkably similar to that of Rogero, confined in a dungeon, surrounded by coffins and death's-heads and crossbones, toads and snails.

Chapter Seven

Breakfast in the Elphinstone household next morning was a lugubrious affair. Drusilla was annoyed that she, along with Lambchop, had not been permitted to attend the theater, and in preference to joining the family at table, remained locked in her bedroom with *The Mysteries of Udolpho*. Ermyntrude, too, was less eager to brave the day than was her custom and greeted the morn with a pout, pulled her pillow over her head, and went back to sleep. As for Sir Geoffrey, if he did not choose to deal with his troubles in quite so cravenly a manner, his emergence from his bedchamber was also tardy, for he was paying for certain excesses of the night before with the devil of a head.

As a result, Tabby was first into the dining room. She seated herself at the mahogany table and surveyed the vast array of food: tea, chocolate, coffee; sausages, kidneys, bacon, toast and muffins, and eggs. Having made her selections, Tabby enlivened her solitude by browsing through a book of household receipts. In some areas, Tabby's education had been shockingly neglected. Her classical studies had not, for example, prepared her to concoct simple medicaments like licorice lozenges or scurvy-grass wine for the consumption of invalids, or to distill rose water or prepare potpourri. Tabby was determined to confront the cook about her consumption of cooking sherry and felt obscurely that it would be to her advantage to know some arcane domestic lore. Overseeing a household of this size was far different from managing her papa's modest staff. Tabby was aware that both above- and belowstairs she was considered a bit of a queer fish.

That couldn't be helped. Tabby took a sip of chocolate and frowned at her book. Certainly none of her past experience had prepared her to combine white flowers, cucumber water, and lemon juice with several plucked and beheaded chickens, all minced fine and digested in an alembic for eighteen days before being utilized to preserve the complexion. Tabby shuddered and pushed away her plate, on which rested a portion of kidneys and eggs.

As she did so, Ermyntrude strolled into the dining room, plucked a muffin from the basket, lavished it with butter, and popped it into her mouth. "It isn't polite to read at table," she said, somewhat unclearly, but with distinct triumph at having caught Tabby in a less-than-perfect act.

Tabby withheld comment. Ermyntrude irritated her today as never before. Even her morning dress of pale yellow muslin, with its frills around the neck, its fluted sleeves and hem, set Tabby's teeth on edge. She told herself to be charitable. Ermyntrude could not have enjoyed seeing the elusive St. Erth cast admiring glances at another woman. "I understand that Mr. Philpotts is very wealthy," she said.

Ermyntrude shrugged and walked toward the window. "He's rich as Croesus—whoever that was! He's also dull as ditch water, and besides, my heart belongs to St. Erth! Even if he is paying attentions that are rather too pointed to that—that lightskirt!"

Tabby remembered the previous evening and how the viscount had stared at the stage. Vivien was used to other gentlemen dangling after Sara, she supposed. Perhaps he would even be amused. As he'd been amused by Tabby herself. Of course it was no more than that. She was not his type, but a plain and awkward bluestocking with nothing to recommend her but her brains, which must be rather despised. "But Miss Divine is, er, in the keeping of another gentleman," she remarked.

Ermyntrude stared. "How do you know that?"

"That sort of woman usually is, I think," Tabby responded vaguely, and returned her attention to her book, where she discovered that one could remove freckles by way of an application of crushed strawberries, green-grape juice, ass's or human milk.

Ermyntrude, too, was silent, as she stared out the window. She employed her usual method of dealing with trouble, by pretending it didn't exist, and counted the passing blue uniforms of the Prince's own regiment, the Tenth Light Dragoons. People spoke poorly of the Tenth, who'd spent the interminable years of the wars with France without setting foot on foreign soil. For her own part, Ermy thought it only right and proper that officers who looked so dashing in their magnificently laced jackets, gold-fringed red breeches, and yellow boots should be spared from nasty battles. "How romantic it would be to elope!" she said aloud. "I should like it above anything. I wonder if St. Erth would be more attentive if I took to wearing false bosoms made of wax, like I saw in *The Lady's Magazine*.

Tabby thought that any gentleman must respond unfavorably to the discovery of such deception. "Whom do you mean to elope with?" she asked, somewhat unkindly.

Ermyntrude turned away from the window. "You're as bad as Dru!" With a toss of red-gold curls, she stamped out of the room.

Tabby finished her chocolate in peace, unmoved by Ermyntrude's displeasure. She was learning how to stew a carp when a footman appeared with a summons from her employer.

Tabby was relieved to be interrupted in her studies and distracted from her foolish thoughts. She pushed back her chair and went in search of Sir Geoffrey.

Drusilla, meanwhile, emerged at last from her bedroom, having grown bored with Mrs. Radcliffe's Gothic castles, persecuted heroines, and tyrannous villains, and set out for the kitchen to make up for her missed meal. The faithful Lambchop padded by her side. As they passed by her papa's study, Drusilla heard his voice. She paused, sorely tempted by the fact that the door was ajar. Lambchop nudged her. Drusilla pushed him aside. At least if she were eavesdropping, then none of the servants could. She positioned herself, somewhat awkwardly, so that she could peer into the room.

Sir Geoffrey's study was a spacious chamber furnished quite handsomely with rosewood and mahogany furniture, comfortable chairs, bookcases adorned with brass inlay with honeysuckle motif. A handsome chandelier descended from the ceiling. Portraits hung on the walls. Sir Geoffrey was seated at a large horseshoe-shaped desk. Tabby sat opposite him on a mahogany armchair of graceful proportions, with fine details of reeding and grooving in its arms and back. Her posture was very stiff. "You wished to speak with me, Sir Geoffrey?" she repeated.

Sir Geoffrey shook his head, as if to clear it. "Ah, Miss Minchin," he said uncomfortably. "Er, why tea leaves and damp sand?"

Tea leaves and damp sand? Whatever Tabby had expected, it was not a query into the more mundane aspects of housekeeping. However, her employer had asked her a question and she must reply. Tabby embarked upon an explanation, with frequent references to the useful volume that she still held in her hand. But Sir Geoffrey was not listening. "You did not summon me here to ask me that, I think," she said.

So he had not. But he didn't know how to broach the subject that he did wish to discuss with Miss Minchin. Sir Geoffrey sighed.

Sir Geoffrey's silence was unnerving. Perhaps he was searching for the words to turn her off? Tabby couldn't bear the suspense. "Is something amiss?" she inquired. "Have I failed to satisfy?"

Sir Geoffrey looked startled. "Why should you think that? You're quite one to the family now, are you not? Our Tabby, abovestairs and below. Why, even my valet speaks highly of you, which I suspect is more than he does me. He says that you're a very knowing puss. Which is what I wished to speak to you about. You are aware of my betrothal to Lady Grey?"

Tabby nodded. She was absurdly touched to learn she'd won the recommendation of Sir Geoffrey's superior valet. As for what success she'd had with the servants, Tabby attributed that less to cleverness than to novelty. They were not accustomed to receiving instruction and responded before they realized what they were about. Too, she was careful not to ask the impossible. But what had this to do with Lady Grey?

Sir Geoffrey was finding explanations difficult. He sat down at his desk and fidgeted with a letter knife. "I'm devoted to Augusta!" he said. "Have been since the day we met. The thing is, she's a devilish high stickler—why, she won't even visit here, because the one time she did, she was shocked at how shabbily we go on. Not that things are not better now!" he added, lest Tabby think he failed to appreciate her efforts. "My tea and toast this morning were quite warm!"

His breakfast had not noticeably benefited Sir Geoffrey; he looked quite worn down. "Thank you," murmured

49

Tabby. She wondered, still, what Sir Geoffrey had wished to talk to her about.

" 'Twas because of Augusta that I hired you," said Sir Geoffrey. "And I got to thinking of how my girls would go on if I suddenly popped off. Of course, it's a somewhat different case, since my pockets aren't to let, but still— And Gus had said any number of times that my girls need a firmer hand on the reins!"

Tabby suspected that the hand Lady Grey had in mind was not a stranger's, but her own. In which case, she must resent Tabby's presence very much. "I hope," Tabby murmured, "that Lady Grey is not displeased."

"Lady Grey is always displeased." Sir Geoffrey threw down his letter knife. "It seems that every time I try to please Gus, I accomplish the opposite! I thought if I didn't have to worry about my girls, I could devote more time to her. And so I might, if she'd come off her high ropes. Gus isn't sure it was proper of me to bring a young girl into a household without a mistress. Although it *will* have a mistress as soon as she can bring herself to set a date!"

Tabby could not help but hope that Lady Grey would not set a date too quickly. It was not inconceivable that her first act as mistress of Elphinstone House would be to turn Tabby off. "Gus's nose is out of joint," added Sir Geoffrey, "because I didn't consult her first. You musn't think we're not well suited. We are, though Gus doesn't realize it yet. She was married right out of the schoolroom to a man old enough to be her father, with principles so lofty they'd make a saint wish to cast up his accounts. It's Grey's fault she's so high in the instep. And he's probably also to blame for her shattered nerves! Not that it signifies. The thing is, there were times before I met her—oh, the devil!" He held out a piece of notepaper. "Perhaps you should read this."

How unhappy Sir Geoffrey looked. Tabby remembered his haunted expression the night before, when she had returned unexpectedly to the box and surprised him staring at the newcomer to St. Erth's box. Tabby had slipped quietly into her seat then, in an attempt to avoid questions about Ermyntrude, and the episode had slipped her mind. Now she gingerly took the highly scented missive from his hand. As she read the scrawled handwriting, her own expression came to resemble his own. "What a pickle!" she said when she had finished. "Who is this Mrs. Quarles?"

Sir Geoffrey pressed his fingers to his temples. "Mrs. Quarles is a devilish ungrateful female, with whom I was, er, friendly before I fell fathoms deep in love with my Gus. And now, apparently, she's gone off her hinges and means to make a cursed nuisance of herself!"

Apparently no Elphinstone was a marvel of discretion. Under other circumstances, Tabby might have laughed to see someone thrown into such a pucker, but she liked Sir Geoffrey too well to be amused at his expense. "I'm sorry," she said gently. "Perhaps if you made a clean breast of the business to Lady Grey—"

Sir Geoffrey looked horrified at the suggestion. "You don't know Gus. If she got into such a flap about my hiring you, can you imagine what she'd say about my association with a—well, Mrs. Quarles has strong passions and indulges them with great latitude, if you take my meaning! Yes, and Gus would have my head on a platter if she could hear me talking to you like this! I know I shouldn't, but I must talk about it or go mad." He dropped his head into his hands. "Damned if I know what I've done to deserve that someone should place an insuperable obstacle in the way of my happiness and endanger my peace of mind!"

Tabby sought some way to console her distrait employer. "Were the letters so very bad? She merely writes that she wishes to speak with you."

"But I don't wish to speak with her!" Sir Geoffrey

51

looked even unhappier as he recalled the throes of his infatuation and how very reckless he had been. "Not only do I not wish to speak with her, you may be sure that if I *did* speak with her, Lady Grey would find out!"

Silence descended upon the study. In the hallway, Drusilla stirred. So fascinated had she been by these disclosures that she had stayed too long in one position and her muscles had grown quite cramped. The name Quarles was not unfamiliar to Drusilla, who, alas, was not above listening to servants' gossip; she associated it with a certain yellow-haired female Sir Geoffrey had doted on a few months past.

In the study, Sir Geoffrey looked at Tabby. "And then I thought of you!"

Why he should have done so Tabby had not the most distant guess. There was no receipt for this kind of trouble in her little book. But she couldn't withstand the hopeful expression on Sir Geoffrey's face. "If there's anything I can do—"

Sir Geoffrey brightened at this offer. He was not wishful of putting a period to his existence, after all. "That's our good Tabby! Clever puss! I knew you would wish to go and meet her in my place! See what she wants and persuade her to go away!"

Drusilla didn't hear Tabby's answer; Lambchop joined her in the hallway then, almost knocking her over in his attempts to display the trophy he'd brought from the kitchen, a cold boiled knuckle of veal. Again, Drusilla pushed him away. Not to be denied his due praise, Lambchop nudged open the study door and collapsed with his booty on the rug.

Drusilla followed her pet into the study. She tugged at his collar, tried to persuade him to dine elsewhere. Lambchop's table manners were appalling and would not benefit the rug. The dog bared his teeth at her in what was doubtless meant to be a friendly gesture and refused to budge. "You'd best give it up," advised Tabby. "Mrs. Phipps didn't, and look what happened."

Drusilla decided that Tabby was unhinged by Sir Geoffrey's confidences. Who the deuce was Mrs. Phipps? "You'd best do as Pa says, Tabby. If Lady Grey finds out about this Quarles female, it'll queer Pa's pitch for sure."

Sir Geoffrey appeared slightly put off by this indication that his younger daughter had been listening at keyholes. "Lady Grey is right!" he said. "I *have* allowed you to run wild. And when this wretched business is cleared up, I shall have a great deal to say to you! But you're right about one thing, puss! If Tabby refuses to act as my emissary, we'll all be in the suds!"

Tabby tried very hard to withstand this pressure. She was growing fond of Sir Geoffrey and his family and wished none of them harm. It seemed very likely that harm would come to them unless someone intervened and tried to convince the dreadful Mrs. Quarles to relinquish all claim to Sir Geoffrey. But why must that someone be her? She glanced desperately around the room in search of rescue. Her gaze fell on Lambchop. Replete, the dog burped and wagged his tail. "Are you going to cry craven?" inquired Drusilla impatiently. "I beg you will not! I'm too young to go and try to reason with this female, and you can imagine what a muddle Ermy would make of it. And it's hardly the sort of thing we can entrust to an outsider, is it, and so you're all that's left!"

Chapter Eight

It was with mixed emotions that Tabby set out from Elphinstone House. Of course she wanted to help Sir Geoffrey. He had rescued her from the prospect of poverty and starvation, after all. To fail to do his bidding now would make her the most undutiful wretch in existence. Only a monster of ingratitude could stand by and see so kind a family disgraced.

Alas, none of these reflections could stop Tabby wishing very fervently that there was someone else who could assist Sir Geoffrey out of his predicament. She was not comfortable with either her assumed role or her borrowed gown—although "borrowed" was not perhaps the proper word for a garment filched from Ermyntrude's wardrobe when that young lady was absent from the house, Drusilla having been adamant that her sister shouldn't be let in on the business, Ermyntrude being far too prone to let cats out of bags. Be that as it may, Tabby could not like the square-necked, low-necked gown of clinging pink muslin, with its short full sleeves. Her petticoats were short enough to expose her ankles rather too frequently, and she felt that her arms and bosom were too much exposed. Maybe she did look quite top of the trees, as Drusilla insisted, but Tabby felt like a silk purse that had been fashioned out of a sow's ear.

She was doing her employer's bidding, Tabby reminded herself. She was present at this gala not as an impostor but as Sir Geoffrey's agent. She was to speak with Mrs. Quarles and persuade that scheming hussy (as Sir Geoffrey had phrased it) to a change of heart. To achieve that purpose, Tabby was armed only with her employer's description of the lady and her own good common sense. It was a very quelling prospect.

Tabby took a deep breath and stepped down from Sir Geoffrey's carriage, walked up to the door. This was her first close view of Brighton Pavilion, so it was only natural that she should stop to stare. Once the Pavilion had been a simple, comfortable seaside house, two stories high, decked externally with nothing more exceptionable than balconies and verandas. But a creative muse—some said demon—had inspired the building's owner to flights of architectural fancy. In the resulting mélange, Tabby thought she recognized elements of Grecian and Gothic, Turkish and Moorish, Egyptian and Chinese and Hindustani. She recovered from her awe and moved toward the entrance.

Invitations to the Pavilion were eagerly sought after, despite the all-too-frequent dullness of the entertainments there, and Tabby was jostled by other guests. For one cowardly moment she hoped she might be turned away by the very superior servants who waited at the door. But such was the influence of Sir Geoffrey, and the good strong elbow of his footman, that she arrived safely within.

The interior of the Pavilion was no less exotic than the exterior. Tabby gazed bemused upon great lacquered panels, red and black and gold; painted and carved dragons that hung from silver ceilings and crawled down pillars; gilded and silvered sofas with dragon motifs; china fishermen that stood in alcoves, with lanterns as their catch. She glimpsed a China gallery, a music room with gorgeous frescoes and green-and-golden dragons, a yellow drawing room with Oriental colonnades, a banqueting hall

55

with domed ceiling representing an Eastern sky. But amidst all this splendor she did not espy a lady answering to Sir Geoffrey's description of his nemesis. And the rooms were insufferably hot. In search of less stale and stifling air, Tabby stepped into an anteroom. She found no opened window there, but instead a gentlemen in the evening dress of the Tenth. He paused in the act of draining a brandy snifter. His slightly glazed expression, as he stared at Tabby, indicated that this glass of liquor was not his first.

How ridiculous he looked. Ermyntrude might admire that magnificently laced jacket, those red breeches with gold fringe, but Tabby found the gentleman reminiscent of an organ-grinder's monkey. "Pray excuse me!" she gasped, attempting to stifle a laugh. "I did not mean to intrude."

But she was not to leave so soon. With a quickness of movement admirable in a gentleman in his cups, the officer placed himself between Tabby and the door. "Something about me amuses you?" he asked.

Tabby did not deem it prudent to inform the gentleman that he reminded her of a performing monkey. "You misunderstood me, sir. It was something else altogether that diverted me. I apologize again for my intrusion. I will leave you now."

The officer was not disposed to let her pass. His bold gaze moved over her body in the clinging muslin dress. The officer was not unhandsome, and more ladies were susceptible to him than not.

Tabby was not among those ladies. Nor was she amused that the officer clearly thought her character equivocal. "You are offensive, sir!" she said coolly. "Pray let me pass."

Still he did not step aside. "I'll show you I'm not to be laughed at!" he said, and grasped her elbows. The man was going to kiss her, Tabby realized. No little bit alarmed, she gazed about for something with which to defend herself. Her choices were limited. Tabby bypassed a lamp shaped like an elegant tulip in favor of a tall porcelain pagoda.

"Unhand me, sir!" she demanded. It seemed only fair that before she began smashing her host's treasures, she give her accostor one last chance. "Release me at once, and we'll say nothing more of this matter, and no harm will be done."

But Tabby's captor was immune to reason, such was the volatile combination of brandy and Ermyntrude's clinging gown. He murmured something unintelligible and drew Tabby closer into his arms. She took firmer grip on the porcelain pagoda, which was amazingly heavy, and prepared to break it over the officer's head.

At that moment, the door swung open. On the threshold stood a green-eyed gentleman. He frowned as he recognized Tabby. "What the *devil*," he inquired, "is going on here?" The officer apparently did not feel up to explanations. He released Tabby and beat a quick retreat.

Tabby wished that she might also do so. What must Vivien think? Probably as had the officer, that she was one of the frail but fair. Tabby meant to have a word with Ermyntrude about her borrowed dress. "Thank you!" she stammered. "For coming to my rescue."

Vivien plucked the pagoda from her hand and returned it to its place. Tabby admired his long-tailed blue coat and black pantaloons, white waistcoat and exquisite cravat. "Prinny is not always wise in his choice of friends," he said. "And, unfortunately, their behavior sometimes leaves much to be desired. Luckily, I was passing by and recognized your voice. Or thought I did." He smiled. "It seemed so bizarre a notion that I had to stop and see."

Bizarre, indeed, thought Tabby. Here she was, a mere dab of a girl, being introduced firsthand to the foibles and indiscretions of the gay and polite. It was not an introduction to which she had aspired. But she could hardly explain to Vivien that she had a job of work to do. "Er, and very glad I am you did!" she responded. "I am in your debt."

"Good!" Vivien smiled again, in a manner calculated to melt the coolest heart. "Then you will not run away from me again so soon! You acted as though you did not trust me when last we met."

Trust this self-admitted rakehell? Of course she did not. But it would be unkind to tell him so. And what on earth was responsible for these sudden palpitations in her chest and the buzzing in her ears?

When she did not answer, Vivien looked concerned. "That brute really upset you, didn't he? The man was drunk. He'll forget you quickly enough. But if it would make you feel better, I'll call him out."

Tabby suffered further palpitations as result of this suggestion and thought of the subsequent notoriety. "Oh, no!" she gasped.

"You relieve me," Vivien said wryly. "I confess I'm not much for pistols at dawn. Is this your first visit to the Pavilion? Come, let me show you around." Tabby could think of no good reason to refuse him. Indeed, she found it curiously comforting that so wicked a person could also be kind. She allowed Vivien to escort her from the room.

He led her down the hallway, stopped a passing servant, presented her with a glass of champagne. Tabby accepted it gratefully, but wrinkled her nose at the bubbles, in a manner that led Vivien to conclude that she wasn't accustomed to strong drink. He didn't know what to make of his Miss Nevermind. At first he'd though her Perry's peculiar, until circumstances had caused him to dismiss that conclusion as absurd. Now he wondered if the notion had been so nonsensical as it had seemed then. In Vivien's experience, no green miss would wear so blatantly inviting a gown. His curiosity was aroused. Vivien was too skilled a sportsman to cram his fences. He did not follow the example set him very recently by a certain officer of the Tenth, but set out on the promised tour, concluding in an astonishing passageway of painted glass, decorated with flowers and insects, fruits and birds, and illuminated from the outside.

Tabby looked around her, awed. It was easy to imagine that they were passing through an immense Chinese garden. And difficult to think why Mrs. Quarles had wished to meet with Sir Geoffrey here. Tabby would have thought a less public setting more suitable for a rendezvous, but she was inexperienced in such things. One thing was certain; the reprehensible Mrs. Quarles had influential friends.

Yes, and Tabby was neglecting her duties. She was here to save her employer and his family from disgrace, not to listen to Vivien describe the stable Prinny was in the process of building, which was to be an equestrian palace with a huge fountain in the center and an exterior in the Moslem Indian style. "I must go!" she said abruptly. "I have already taken up too much of your time."

"You must let me be the judge of that." Vivien had half expected such a maneuver; he caught her hand. "I rescued you, did I not? You have not offered me a reward."

Tabby flushed as she realized what sort of reward a rakehell would demand. She tried to ignore the warmth of his hand, which was disturbing even through the fabric of her glove. "So I am forfeit?" she said lightly. "It does not seem entirely chivalrous of you to demand a reward."

"Chivalrous?" Vivien quirked a brow. "You forget my reputation. It was not by being chivalrous that I earned my name."

"Nor is it by being chivalrous that you live up to it, I gather!" Tabby retorted wryly. "I begin to think myself doubly fortunate that you interfered with that odious officer on my behalf."

Vivien stroked the palm of her hand with his thumb. "Chivalry played no part here, either, my dear. I could not stand by and watch another man take what I wanted myself."

Here was plain spokenness! Tabby stared at the marble floor. Then she realized that, of course, he was not serious. "You are in a very teasing mood, I think!" she murmured.

In a teasing mood, was he? Vivien glanced down the passageway. The other guests having withdrawn to the banqueting rooms to discover what culinary delights awaited, he and Tabby had the Oriental hallway to themselves. It made a very romantic setting. "No, I do not jest," he said, and moved his hands to cup her face.

He was going to kiss her. Tabby knew that she should flee. But common sense was flanked by the combined effects of champagne and Ermyntrude's reckless gown. Vivien's hand moved over her bare shoulders, her arms. She shivered.

Her bemused expression was absurdly touching. "Come away with me," Vivien said huskily. "Now."

Where did he want her to go? Tabby wished she might find out. But honor demanded that she carry out her duty to Sir Geoffrey. "I cannot," she said.

Vivien's hands tightened. "Why not? You'll want for nothing. If there's some, er, impediment, I'll buy him off."

Tabby blinked. "Good God! You're offering me carte blanche!" she said.

Vivien was not accustomed to having his offers of patronage greeted with astonishment. "I've made a mistake, it appears," he said, and released her. "Pray accept my apologies."

How cross he looked. Tabby thought Vivien seldom blundered in matters such as this. "Don't regard it!" she said kindly. "It is no wonder that you thought I was a bit o'—that you thought what you did! This dreadful gown would lead anyone to that conclusion, and my own behavior was not, well, er!''

Vivien was charmed by her confusion. ''Shall we cry pax?'' he said. ''I have both rescued and abused you, so perhaps we may now be friends.''

''I should like that.'' Tabby glanced shyly up at him. ''You did not abuse me so very much, you know.''

Vivien knew that he would like to abuse her further, so winsome did she look. He was spared putting his willpower to the test by the sound of a distant voice calling his name. Tabby recognized that voice also. She looked wildly about her, as if she might seek refuge behind an illusory Chinese tree.

''Wait!'' Vivien caught her wrist. ''We are friends now, so you must trust me a little bit. Won't you tell me who you are?''

Quite naturally, Tabby did no such thing—although, truth be told, her reticence sprang less from a desire to protect her employer and his family than from a desire to spare herself the mortification that such a confession must bring. If Vivien were to think of her again, unlikely as the prospect seemed, let him remember her as a woman of mystery rather than a lowly governess embarked on a charade.

Sara's voice came closer. ''Vivien!'' She sounded as though she would momentarily appear around the bend of the hallway.

''Oh, please!'' gasped Tabby. ''You must let me go!''

Vivien knew he must release her, for both their sakes. Did Sara discover them together, nothing would prevent her from raising an almighty fuss. But he would not give up his advantage. ''Your name!'' he said again.

He demanded a name? Then Tabby must give him one. But what, if not her own? And not Elphinstone?

"Vivien!" Sara's voice came closer still; her footsteps echoed down the hall. "Quarles!" gasped Tabby. Vivien released her, and she fled.

Chapter Nine

Lady Grey was taking the waters, for reasons of her health. Sea bathing in Brighton was a serious affair, to be undertaken with medical supervision, and was prescribed for all manner of chronic complaints, asthma and deafness and consumption, rheumatism and ruptures and madness—and, in lady Grey's case, afflicted nerves. One hired a machine, in which one could disrobe privately and don a flannel smock. Then one was pulled out into the water by a horse, and descended from the machine into the water in the strictest seclusion. It was a popular procedure, engaged in occasionally even by royalty. The story was still told of how, when Prinny had gone in too far, his dipper had to drag him in to shore by the ear.

Lady Grey intensely disliked the whole business. The bathing machines had no awnings, and she was convinced that the gentlemen with their telescopes trained on the shoreline were much less interested in the antics of the fishing fleet than in the beflannelled ladies splashing in the muddy margins of the sea. She was equally convinced that taking the waters had not benefited her nerves. If anything, the sojourn had made them worse. She made a final adjustment to her bonnet, her gray walking dress. Her obligation to her physician fulfilled, she exited the bathing establishment and stepped into the sunlight.

Wood's Bath was situated within a few yards of William's New Bath, near the fish market on the Steyne. Lady Grey averted her gaze from the gentlemen clad for their early morning baths in buff trousers and slight jackets, who shockingly lounged about in this state of undress for all the world to see, and glanced toward the market stalls. A certain gentleman engaged in a transaction at the fish stall attracted her interest. He beckoned to her. Lady Grey ignored him and quickly set out at a good pace.

Along the Steyne, she traveled; past shops displaying toys and rare china, lace and ribbons and millinery, muslins and chintzes and cambrics, and tea. Neither the parish church nor the Chapel Royal aroused her interest; she did not pause even for Mr. Donaldson's library, where customers sat under the colonnades reading the London newspapers and watching fashionable Brighton pass by. But then a plaintive voice caught her attention. "I say, Gus! I wish you would slow down, because I can't stand the pace. That sea bathing seems to be the ticket! Maybe I should take the waters myself."

Lady Grey loathed her nickname and had once boxed her younger brother's ears for daring to address her in that way. From this source, however, she accepted the detested familiarity. There was satisfaction, also, in the fact that he had trailed after her all this way. She turned.

Sir Geoffrey smiled. He bore his ladylove no malice, for all she'd led him a merry chase. Gad, but his Gus was a lovely creature, with her bright green eyes and pale fair skin and hair. "Have I put your back up again?" he inquired ruefully. "Because, if not, I have not the least distant guess why you should run away from me!"

Lady Grey flushed with embarrassment. "I do not mean to be contrariwise! Pray forgive me. It is just that—"

"My dear, it is I who must apologize." Sir Geoffrey was charmed by his Gus's confusion. He shifted the package that he held, thus bringing it to her attention. It was a very sloppily wrapped package, tied with string, and the aroma that clung to it left little doubt as to what was within.

Augusta wrinkled her delicate nose. "Gracious, Geoffrey! Are you doing the household shopping now? It is what I might expect from your daughters, but I wonder that your Miss—what *was* her name?—would allow such a thing."

Sir Geoffrey drew Lady Grey's hand through his arm, guided her toward the seawall that did double duty as an esplanade. "Miss Minchin is a clever little miss. A taking little thing. I make no doubt she'll take us in hand!" He chuckled at his joke.

Lady Grey did not join in his laugher, permitted herself only a wan little smile. Her silence was comment in itself, and Sir Geoffrey studied her pale face. "It is very good of you to concern yourself about my girls. They are a thought high-spirited, I know."

A thought high-spirited? Lady Grey could not let this gross understatement pass. "Ermyntrude," she said bluntly, "is making an exhibition of herself in the neighborhood. You've raised your daughter from the cradle, Sir Geoffrey. Can't you stop her throwing herself at St. Erth?"

How Sir Geoffrey disliked conversations of this nature. He was an amiable man and made unhappy by upsets. It occurred to him, not for the first time, that his Gus was frequently in a deuced touchy frame of mind. He murmured vaguely about letting nature take its course. "Anyway, I don't think I *did* raise her! Seems to me like Ermy and Dru raised themselves." He smiled. "You worry too much. My girls will be right as a trivet. As for Ermy's tendre for St. Erth—why, look about you! Love is in the air."

Among her countless virtues, Lady Grey did not include a sense of humor. Taking Sir Geoffrey's injunction seriously, she gazed about the esplanade. Brighton was popular

65

at this time of year. The esplanade was thronged with people strolling on foot, riding on horseback and in coach, traveling in bath carriages. Beyond the esplanade lay the beach itself, where children queued up for a donkey ride while their elders made use of the bathing machines. Nothing in Gus's surroundings reminded her of Cupid, except Sir Geoffrey himself. He appeared deep in thought.

Lady Grey took advantage of her fiancé's abstraction to subject him to a covert inspection. He was tall and handsome, with those classic features and blue eyes and red-gold hair and the physique of a man much younger than his forty years. Augusta sighed. Each day she hoped to find Sir Geoffrey less attractive and herself less susceptible to his good looks. To date, that hope had been in vain. He was rendered no less handsome even by the smelly fish he held, as was evident from the number of ladies who gazed appreciatively upon him as they strolled past. Lady Grey had never felt this way before, certainly not about her deceased husband, who'd been chosen for her by her parents and had been a great deal older than she. It seemed to her inappropriate that she should fall in love for the first time at her age, and with someone about those whose character she had grave reservations. She thought of Ermyntrude. At least at five-and-thirty one might hope to have more worldly wisdom than at seventeen.

Sir Geoffrey caught her gaze. Gus looked unhappy, and so he thrust his own worries away. "There's no need to be troubling your pretty head about Ermy!" he repeated. "She'll do just fine. I make no doubt Miss Minchin will have both my girls up to snuff in no time! Already, she's settled in and become quite one of the family."

Lady Grey valiantly withheld the opinion that it would take the intervention of the Almighty to convert Sir Geoffrey's hoyden daughters into pattern cards of respectability, after their papa had left them to run wild for so long. And as for this Miss Minchin whom he considered such a paragon— "I hope you may not have to repent of your choice," Augusta said repressively.

Sir Geoffrey wished his Gus wasn't quite so high a stickler. "Come down off your high ropes, Gus! Next you'll accuse Miss Minchin of being a serpent clasped to my bosom. Let me assure you that the only thing I've clasped to my bosom of late is you, and that not half so often as I'd like!"

Augusta flushed. Shocking as it was in her, she wished the opportunity for clasping arose more often than it did. "Oh, dear, was I being—"

"Starched-up?" supplied Sir Geoffrey. "It don't signify." His long acquaintance with the family weakness had gained him a certain insight where feminine feelings were concerned. Lady Grey's sense of decorum would not allow her to admit that her pride had been wounded by his failure to consult with her. Seldom did Gus slip and show him her true feelings. He was gratified.

But he did not wish her to be made unhappy, and the matter of Miss Minchin had obviously caused her distress. "Should I not have hired Miss Minchin? Do you wish me to turn her off?"

"Gracious, no!" Augusta protested nobly, although she wasn't certain she didn't wish just that. "You must do what you think best, of course."

What a paragon his Gus was—or tried to be. Sir Geoffrey smiled. "Let me introduce you to Miss Minchin," he suggested. "You may see for yourself that she's a well-brought-up young woman, puss. Fallen on hard times."

Fallen into clover, rather. Lady Grey could not imagine that the duties required of Miss Minchin would prove arduous. "Ah, yes, I must meet Miss Minchin," she said vaguely. Could Augusta have met Miss Minchin in that moment, she might well have succumbed to an unbecoming violence of feeling and boxed the scheming hussy's ears.

Perhaps the sound of the waves pounding on the soft white cliffs was giving his beloved one of her frequent headaches? How charmingly absurd it was of Gus to take a pet. "A mere slip of a girl!" Sir Geoffrey said reassuringly. "She can't hold a candle to you, puss!"

Lady Grey roused from her abstraction. "I don't care a fig for Miss Minchin!" she snapped. "Look! Why on earth is that female making such an exhibition of herself? Can she be trying to attract our attention, do you think?"

It was with no particular foreboding that Sir Geoffrey turned to discover what had aroused Gus's interest. Assuming that Tabby had successfully carried out the duty he'd assigned her, he had been feeling free from much alarm.

"She *is* waving at us!" marveled Lady Grey. "How very queer. I'm sure I've never seen the woman before in my life!" She narrowed her eyes. "Or I think I have not, although it is very difficult to tell in that absurd hat!"

It was indeed a large hat, decorated in a very fanciful style, and obscured not only its wearer's face but hid her hair. Still, Sir Geoffrey had no difficulty recognizing the hat's owner. He wasn't certain he didn't also recognize the hat. Perhaps it was among a number of similar concoctions for which he had stood the bill.

Lady Grey's suspicions were aroused by Sir Geoffrey's silence. She hoped she might not be called vulgarly inquisitive, but surely any woman must be a teeny bit curious to see her fiancé's eyes starting out of his head. "Geoffrey! That woman is trying to get *your* attention!" she said.

Sir Geoffrey gave up his efforts to steer Lady Grey in a different direction. Amazing how even the frailest and most pliant female could, given the right provocation, become as unmovable as a tree. "A trifling matter!" he said feebly. "Tabby was supposed to attend to it—yes, and I shall know why she did not!"

Gus could not be displeased that Miss Minchin had failed to satisfy. However, at this moment her attention was largely for the woman in the absurd hat, who was withdrawing from her reticule what appeared to be a note. The woman stopped an urchin, pointed at Sir Geoffrey, handed the child the missive and a coin.

"How very strange!" said Lady Grey. "If the woman wishes to speak to you, why doesn't she simply do so? This clandestine behavior is hardly what one likes!"

Sir Geoffrey, as he watched this little drama, considered his options. The earth would not open and swallow him, and he was not sufficiently a coward to flee. The urchin approached, held out the note. Lady Grey snatched it from the child's hand.

Her pale complexion turned even more ashen as she read. " 'Have you forgot so soon that I conceded you the ultimate favor!' " she gasped. "Geoffrey, who is this Mrs. Quarles? Do not bother answering; I'm sure I do not care! You will see, I think, that I have no choice but to declare our betrothal at an end!"

This time, Sir Geoffrey made no effort to follow Lady Grey as she stalked haughtily down the esplanade. He bent and picked up the note from the ground where she had let it fall and tucked it into the packet of fish. Then he set out homeward, with the intention of blowing out his brains.

Chapter Ten

The kitchen was a busy place, where maidservants assisted in the cook's culinary efforts, pounding and scrubbing and chopping, polishing the copper cooking utensils and the cooking range. It was an area of the house that Drusilla particularly liked, despite the fact that the lower floor was badly ventilated and overly warm. She enjoyed the bustle and the cooking smells and the gossip she overheard there.

This day, however, there was no gossip to overhear, only Tabby quarreling with the cook. At first they seemed to be arguing about the best way to stew carp. Then the debate turned to the tin traps set about the room to entice the black beetles that liked to congregate there. Cook averred that the traps should be baited with brown sugar, then plunged into hot water when the insects ventured within. Tabby seemed to think that cooking sherry would be more to the point, which made no sense to Drusilla, nor apparently to the kitchen maids, who looked bewildered as result of the exchange. Lambchop created a diversion, then, edging too close to the roast that was intended for the evening meal and causing the cook to snatch angrily at a broom.

"Tabby, I must talk to you!" Drusilla cried, as she hurriedly exited the kitchen in the wake of her pet. Tabby's

70

reformatory zeal was temporarily frustrated by Lambchop's ill manners and Cook's resultant fury. She followed Drusilla up the stairs into the drawing room, where Lambchop collapsed on the Brussels rug.

Tabby sat on a parlor chair of brass-inlaid rosewood. "What was it you wished to speak to me about?"

"As if you didn't know!" Drusilla dropped down beside her pet on the floral-patterned carpet. "Pa trusted you, Tabby, and you have let him down, and after he was good enough to give you a place here! And after I went to all the trouble to filch one of Ermy's gowns. Just what did you *do* at the party? You wasn't sent there to have fun!"

"No, nor did I!" retorted Tabby, who was made very cross by this ingratitude. "Nor did I find—"

"Well!" a third voice interrupted wrathfully from the window seat. "*Well*! Filched my gown, did you, Dru? So that Tabby here might keep an assignation, which is even worse! I don't suppose it occurred to you that in my gown she might be mistook for *me*!"

This notion had occurred to neither Drusilla nor Tabby, both of whom now looked blank. "Tabby don't bear the least resemblance to you," Drusilla pointed out. "She's shorter and rounder, and furthermore, her hair ain't red."

"My hair isn't red!" protested Ermyntrude. "It's gold! And if someone were nearsighted, they might make such an error, queer as it might seem. I have decided St. Erth must be nearsighted. Did you see him at your party, Tabby? Did he pay you particular attention, thinking you was me?"

Tabby thought of the gentleman who had paid her particular attention. "To the best of my knowledge, St. Erth wasn't there."

"Don't try to bamboozle me!" Ermyntrude stamped her little foot. "I know perfectly well he wasn't in his rooms last evening!"

"Are you spying on him now?" Drusilla was diverted

71

from her annoyance with Tabby by this indication that her sister's misbehavior had been even worse. "You'd do better to have Philpotts, Ermy. He'll wear better in the end."

"Never!" Ermyntrude shuddered. "I ask you, who could cherish tender feelings for a man with such a name as Osbert Philpotts?" She turned to Tabby for confirmation. "Could you?"

Tabby thought that damsels who lived in glass houses shouldn't throw stones. Before she could frame a tactful response, Ermyntrude had turned away. "I am quite victim to my heart. It is the family weakness! But neither of you would know about such things."

Drusilla grimaced meaningfully at Tabby. "It makes me cross as crabs to hear her go on like this. When I think—well, I'm only thirteen, and Ermy was tolerable when she was thirteen, but look at her now!"

Tabby did glance at Sir Geoffrey's elder daughter. Ermyntrude's expression was pensive. When she became aware that four eyes rested on her—six, counting Lambchop's—she roused. "A particularly elegant, handsome man!" she sighed. "A very Apollo in form! The curl of his handsome mouth—the way his curls tumble forward on his brow!"

This description, not surprisingly, reminded Tabby of a certain rakehell. Surely Vivien wouldn't be so very wicked as to trifle with a lovely pea-goose like Ermyntrude! But he had been willing enough to trifle with a plump little nobody like Tabby herself. Oh, why was she thinking of him now? But still she could not refrain from asking, "Who?"

Drusilla rolled her eyes. "Who else? Lionel, Viscount St. Erth! Ermy wants to lead St. Erth into parson's mousetrap, but it's clear he don't care a button for what she wants."

How foolish Tabby had been. And how relieved that one

of her charges hadn't somehow been exposed to the wicked Vivien.

Ermyntrude was glowering at her sister. "I am *not* on the dangle for St. Erth! It is St. Erth who has a distinguishing preference for me."

"To be sure he does," Drusilla retorted. "He just ain't discovered it yet. Don't be such a goose, Ermy! Maybe St. Erth would be a fine catch for any miss, but you've been throwing out lures ever since you first clapped eyes on him, and it looks to me like he's less enraptured than downright indifferent."

"And what would you know about it?" So indignant was Ermyntrude made by this calumny that she abandoned her indolent posture on the ottoman to pace with some agitation around the room. "Throwing out lures, indeed! You'll make Tabby think I'm a complete flirt." She turned to Tabby. "Dru is just a child! You musn't pay her any heed. It utterly sinks my spirits that she is such a gudgeon on the subject of St. Erth!"

Tabby's own spirits were of a somewhat melancholy cast. Each further moment passed in Sir Geoffrey's household made her wonder if, in being so eager to take a position, she had not jumped from the frying pan into the fire. "A gudgeon, am I?" retorted Dru. "Very well, Ermy, I'll make you a wager! Gran's pearls that you can't bring St. Erth up to snuff!"

"Done!" cried Ermyntrude, without hesitation. "Though why Gran left her baubles to you in the first place, I have never understood!"

"Mayhap she liked me better," Drusilla suggested. Ermyntrude's cheeks flamed. "This is fair and far off, Ermy! You might try to think of other people once in a while. Here we are trying to pull Pa's coals out of the fire, and instead of trying to help, you do your best to add fuel to the flame!"

"I don't know what you're talking about," Ermyntrude

said sulkily. "And I don't see how it's going to pull anyone's coals out of the fire to send Tabby off to keep assignations in my place!"

"It wasn't in your place," interjected Tabby, before Ermyntrude and Drusilla could get to dagger drawing once again. "It had nothing to do with you, Ermyntrude!"

Ermyntrude wasn't easily sidetracked. "Of course it had to do with me!" she snapped. "It was my gown you wore! And you may bamboozle Dru into thinking you were doing Pa some favor, but you shan't bamboozle me. You were having an assignation of your own!"

"Nonsense!" Tabby responded sternly. "And since you will not leave the subject, I wish to speak to you about that gown. It's not at all the thing for a girl your age. Indeed, for a girl of any age, unless she's a demirep! I'm surprised your papa does not forbid you to wear it. He must realize it will give any gentleman who sees you in it the wrong idea."

"Not the wrong idea!" said Ermyntrude, further incensed by this intimation of the gown's success. "And how would you know about all that unless some gentleman had got the wrong idea about you? Which no gentleman would have if you hadn't filched my dress! You needn't deny it! I know the signs."

So did Drusilla know the signs. She stared in dismay at Tabby's rosy cheeks. If Cupid's dart had smitten even the practical Tabby, there was no hope Drusilla might escape.

Firmly, Tabby banished the image of a green-eyed rakehell from her mind. "I am not of a romantic nature. My mama was, you see, and ran off when I was very young, leaving my papa and me to rub on without her as best we could."

Ermyntrude wore a faraway expression. "Just fancy. A carefree life of dissipation. Flitting from flower to flower." She became aware of the consternated expressions turned toward her and forced a laugh. "Sillies! I was only bamming you."

Tabby hoped that Ermyntrude was indeed teasing. "That sort of thing is not so amusing at firsthand," she responded quietly. "It is the families who suffer when someone throws her bonnet over the windmill."

"Yes, and it's also the families who suffer when someone blows out their brains!" Drusilla interjected brutally. "Which is what runs in *our* family. Uncle Willard swallowed his peas off his knife, then used it to slit his wrists. Not that anyone could blame him, because he was married to Aunt Hester, and she used to remove her false teeth at table and rinse her mouth with water in front of us all!"

Ermyntrude looked impressed. "Fancy you remembering that! You were barely out of the cradle then."

"How could I forget?" Drusilla hugged Lambchop. "I thought Pa was the greatest beast in nature because he wouldn't let me have false teeth of my own."

Ermyntrude studied her companions, both of whom appeared to be in the dumps. In perfect reverse proportions, her own mood improved. "How the two of you do go on," she said. "What about Pa? Why should his coals need hauling from the fire?"

Tabby recalled guiltily that Drusilla had wished to speak to her about that very matter. "Yes, what's happened now? Why is it so dreadful that I was unable to speak to Mrs. Quarles?"

Drusilla extracted a folded square of notepaper from her bodice. At the smell of fish, Lambchop roused. Drusilla fended off her pet. "Hang it!" said Tabby, as she recognized the notepaper. "I mean, she is the most letter-writing female!"

"What female? Who is this Mrs. Quarles?" Ermyntrude plucked the missive from Drusilla's hand. What a queer scent clung to it. Frowning, Ermyntrude struggled to decipher the handwriting. Then her eyes widened, and

75

she sat down plump on a zebrawood sofa. " 'Conceded the ultimate favor'—oh, gracious! Who'd have thought that Pa—"

Drusilla retrieved the note before Lambchop could make a feast of it. "Apparently Lady Grey didn't have any trouble thinking so! She cried off. But Pa'll be all right for a time yet; I've hidden his dueling pistols and dosed him with laudanum! Yes, and he is just the sort of gudgeon who would blow his brains out! He says he can't live without Lady Grey, but Lady Grey's nerves won't stand a scandal, so— I suppose it's the family weakness that prompted Pa to indulge in a torrid love affair with the sort of female who'd later proved deuced indiscreet!" There was nothing for it then, of course, but that she must explain the whole. At the conclusion of her account, both Tabby and Ermyntrude were pale.

Ermyntrude spoke first. "We must do something! Poor Pa!"

For once, Drusilla found herself in agreement with her sister. She left off hugging Lambchop, for which the dog was grateful; due to the severity of her emotional disturbance, Drusilla's caress had felt more like a stranglehold. Lest she be tempted to similarly abuse him again, Lambchop moved away from her and collapsed across Tabby's feet.

"Tabby was supposed to do something!" said Drusilla. "She was supposed to meet this Quarles female and talk sense to her last night! It's obvious Pa can't talk to her, because if he's threatening to blow his brains out, he might decide also to blow out that female's, did he meet her face-to-face. And if Lady Grey won't stand for his old amours being brought to light, think what she would say about his shooting one! I'm disappointed in you, Tabby! Disaster threatens us—Pa disgraced, Ermy and me left fatherless, and you without a place. All of us brought to a standstill because you wouldn't help. And, Ermy, I vow I shall

76

scream if I hear one more word about your dress, so be quiet and let me think!''

Ermyntrude obeyed this injunction, and Tabby was lost in her own thoughts, so all was quiet for a space of time. Ermyntrude gazed out the window into the street, while Drusilla nibbled on her thumb. Meanwhile, Tabby tried to convince herself that it was not her fault Sir Geoffrey was in the devil of a pickle and failed. If she had not run away from Vivien, she might have contrived to speak with Mrs. Quarles, might have persuaded the woman not to write the note that had been read, with such disastrous results, by Lady Grey. It seemed to Tabby that she had behaved in a very cowardly and ungrateful way. She wriggled her toes under Lambchop's bulk. The dog was hot on her feet and was probably shedding his fur all over her dress, as well as imbibing it with a distinctly doggy smell; but Tabby took comfort from the contact.

That contact gave her renewed courage—or perhaps foolishness. "Perhaps it might help," she ventured, "if I spoke with Lady Grey."

Chapter Eleven

Tabby set out through the streets of Brighton, past buildings that were gaily painted and plastered as if to make up for the local absence of timber and stone. Her destination was Lady Grey's lodging on the Royal Crescent. Tabby might have undertaken to meet her own executioner with more enthusiasm than she did her task. Still, something must be done about this dreadful muddle, and Tabby could think of no other step. Surely Lady Grey would not be impervious to reason. If she cared for her fiancé, she would not be eager to believe the worst. She might well lend her efforts to achieving some happy resolution of the current troubles. Heaven knew, Tabby would welcome assistance from any source. Surely Lady Grey was not so unreasonable as she had been made out. The Elphinstones were prone to exaggeration, as Tabby knew well. Having mustered as optimistic a frame of mind as was possible, she walked up to Lady Grey's front door.

The footman who answered Tabby's summons was not welcoming. "Lady Grey is not at home,' he said haughtily, and made to close the door. Tabby thwarted him with an inventiveness born of desperation. "Lady Grey must be in!" she cried. "She is expecting me to call."

The footman raised his brows fractionally higher. "The mistress isn't expecting anyone!" he retorted. "She told me so herself! At the same time she told me to turn away anyone who came calling, because she wasn't up to receiving visitors." He looked suspicious. "Particularly if their name was Elphinstone!"

Tabby decided not to send word to Lady Grey that Sir Geoffrey's governess was here. Rather, his daughters' governess, though Tabby felt at this particular moment that Sir Geoffrey was her most troublesome charge. She might smile now to remember how she had worried about her ability to instruct the Misses Elphinstone in such commonplace topics as grammar and geography and the gloves; might even think wistfully of employers who required a governess to spend her spare moments stitching a tidy seam. But the footman was preparing to close the door in her face. "Maybe Lady Grey is not precisely expecting me," Tabby said quickly, "but she should have known I'd call. Tell her—tell her I must speak to her regarding a very delicate matter. I can say no more at the moment, but also mention to her the name Quarles."

The footman's jaw dropped open. Lady Grey's high principles did not prevent the servants in her employ from enjoying a gossip about their betters as well as any other members of their class. The footman had not been surprised to learn that Sir Geoffrey had a wandering eye; it was not a prerogative solely of the upper class. The footman had a bit of an eye for the ladies himself. But he *was* astonished at the temerity of this female walking right up to the front door. And he was even more astonished at her appearance. "Quarles!" he repeated. "Cor!"

Tabby wondered why the footman was staring so at her. She took advantage of his befuddlement to walk past him into the entry hall. "Shouldn't you inform your mistress that I am here?" she asked.

The footman didn't know what he should do, so thunderstruck was he. This bizarre situation must be referred to his superiors, posthaste. Perhaps the butler would have an opinion, or the housekeeper. "Follow me, ma'am." He abandoned Tabby in a small anteroom as he fled for help.

Tabby didn't mind being left alone; it gave her an opportunity to collect her thoughts and marshal her arguments. Lady Grey must be brought to realize that Sir Geoffrey, above all, was good and generous and kind. Perhaps he was also a trifle foolish, but that did not signify, surely, in light of his other excellent qualities? Tabby sighed. It would be difficult to convince Lady Grey of something she didn't believe herself. Tabby didn't think she'd want a husband who was foolish, no matter how generous and kind. Not that she was likely to have a husband of any nature now. But this was no fit moment in which to mourn her spinster state, particularly since a tall and very superior-looking female had walked into the anteroom and was looking disapprovingly at her. So disapprovingly that Tabby wondered if she had a rip or a smudge. "Lady Grey?" she asked, though she knew it could not be. By all accounts, Lady Grey was as beautiful as she was disagreeable.

The woman's long nose twitched. "I'm Grimsley," she said. Very fortunate it was that the shaken footman had encountered Grimsley; she had more opinions than the butler and housekeeper combined. "Her ladyship's abigail. Herself sent me to fetch you." She walked down the hallway and up the stair, leaving Tabby to keep up as best she could. So brisk was Grimsley's pace that Tabby was breathless when the abigail stopped outside a door. "Herself's within," she said, and stepped back a pace.

Tabby stared at the closed door and then at Grimsley. The abigail looked wooden, a task to which her harsh features were suited admirably. Tabby took a deep breath, turned the door handle and walked into the room, taking a somewhat unchristian pleasure in closing the door in Grimsley's face.

80

The room was in shadow, the draperies drawn. Tabby paused just inside the doorway while her eyes adjusted to the dim light. All was quiet except for the ticking of an ormolu clock on the mantelpiece. Tabby wondered if the abigail had led her to the wrong room.

Lady Grey had the advantage; her own eyes were accustomed to the gloom. She stared at the intruder, who stood so very far away that her features were indistinct. From this distance, she didn't look the sort of female who—who would wear that absurd hat. At least she'd had sufficient sensibility to adapt a more subdued fashion for her visit here. A pity her sensibility hadn't been sufficiently exquisite to keep her away altogether! Augusta rose abruptly from the daybed upon which she had been resting and flung open the drapes.

As sunlight so suddenly poured into the room, Tabby gasped. "Goodness, but you startled me! I had thought I was quite alone." Still the woman silhouetted against the bright window did not speak. "Lady Grey?" Tabby asked doubtfully.

Augusta was also feeling doubtful. She had broached a bottle of her deceased spouse's excellent claret—not that she was a secret tippler; wine-and-water was known to be an excellent headache cure—and now wondered if the liquor had adversely affected her eyesight. The intruder looked absurdly young, but Gus's far vision had never been good. Certainly the liquor had affected her reasoning abilities. Gus's initial response to this intrusion was curiosity. "I have a headache," she said, and vaguely waved the dampened handkerchief that had lain across her brow. "Come closer, do!"

So peremptory was that tone of voice that Tabby instantly obeyed. She felt like an applicant for a post, under Lady Grey's stern gaze. Obviously Lady Grey realized that she was the Elphinstone governess. That was one explanation saved.

"I would have expected you to be more, er, flamboyant," remarked Lady Grey. "Perhaps that hat was a single aberration in good taste. Not that you are to be commended for your current course of action. Tell me, I do entreat you, what purpose you think to accomplish here?"

What hat? wondered Tabby. The stench of eau de cologne in the small room was enough to give anyone a headache. "I wished to speak to you," she responded. "In Sir Geoffrey's behalf."

"In Sir Geoffrey's—" So startled was Lady Grey by this information that she sank back down on her daybed. "I never heard of such a thing!"

Lady Grey had more in common with the Elphinstones than Tabby had imagined, including a certain incomprehensibility of speech. "Sir Geoffrey is in a sad way," she persisted. "He is so unhappy that we fear for his health. I do not mean to presume, but I fear you have done him a great disservice, ma'am."

"A great disservice," echoed Lady Grey. Her initial shock—a less kind person might say inebriation—was wearing off, and a vast anger was taking its place. How dare this brazen hussy accost her in her own home and accuse her of acting shabbily? With her back to the bright window, so Augusta still had no clear notion of her features?

That at least would change. With resolution Lady Grey abandoned her daybed, strode across the room, and grasped the intruder by the arm. At last she had a clear view of her rival's face.

Augusta stared. "Gracious!" she said weakly. "You're just a child. The man must be mad. He looks mad. I thought so just the other day when I told him that our betrothal was at an end."

Tabby thought that not only Sir Geoffrey's powers of logic were in question. Like called to like, after all. But clearly Lady Grey doubted her qualifications and must be reassured. "I am not so very young!" Tabby said hastily. "And youth is not always a disadvantage, you know! I am perhaps more flexible than an older woman in my position—more able to adjust to new situations. I am not so young that I cannot give satisfaction, I promise you!"

Lady Grey was overwhelmed by such outspokenness. She released Tabby and fumbled for her vinaigrette. "Depraved! The man is positively depraved!" she gasped.

"Oh, surely not!" Tabby was mystified to know what had inspired Lady Grey's outburst. "If he has misbehaved, it is nothing so terribly bad, because the gentlemen will occasionally do that which we would rather they did not, you know!"

Lady Grey did not know, nor did she wish to, nor did she doubt Tabby's ability to present her with numerous accounts of errant gentlemen, complete in every detail. "I beg I may hear of no such thing!" she cried. "Such vice in one so young—it's Geoffrey's fault, of course! What a monster of depravity he is, to first, er, take advantage of you and then send you here to intercede for him!"

Sir Geoffrey had taken advantage of her? Tabby supposed he had. Lady Grey was certainly prone to see things in the worst possible light. "You put too fine a point on it," she protested. "Perhaps matters appear a trifle irregular, but had not Sir Geoffrey come to my rescue, my situation would have been much too dreadful to contemplate. But I did not come here to speak of myself. Pray reconsider your decision, Lady Grey. Sir Geoffrey is so unhappy that I fear he may go into a decline."

She was expected to care about Geoffrey's well-being? So far as Augusta was concerned, that vilest of seducers could sink speedily into the bowels of hell. She had been right to have reservations about him. What a fool he had made of her! At her age she should have known better than to believe his pretty blandishments. Augusta experienced a sense of burning resentment at the easy, skillful manner in which he'd led her astray.

The last cobwebs of sleep and claret were dissipated now by her resentment. "Hussy!" she cried. "Trollop! What gall you exhibit in coming here, what colossal nerve! But I am not surprised; I know of your sort! Not that I am accustomed to entertaining bits o' muslin in my house!"

Tabby stared at Lady Grey. "Good God!" she said. "You think that *I*—"

"I don't think!" interrupted Lady Grey, with admirable accuracy. "I *know*! I hope I am not one to kick up a dust over trifles, but I find myself totally unable to swallow this with a good grace. Oh, why did you come here? As if that were not improper enough, then you forced me to listen to you, instead of having immediately had you shown the door. And now you will bandy *that* all about the town, as well as the other, and I shall seem little better than one of the wicked myself, in addition to being a laughingstock!"

Lady Grey made a pathetic figure, dropping on her daybed, a sight pitiful enough to wring the hardest heart. Tabby might well have pitied the woman, had not the suggestion that she was Sir Geoffrey's *petite amie* inspired her with the giggles. "It is a misunderstanding!" she gasped. "I'm not! How could you think— Oh! Because of the name Quarles!"

"You're laughing!" Augusta was pink with outrage. "You're laughing! Have you no sensibility, you horrid thing?"

Tabby choked back her laughter. "Well, no, I don't think I must!" she confessed. "Which is as well for all concerned, since it is apparently up to me to see that this muddle is cleared up. If you will forgive my plainspokenness, Lady Grey, you have treated Sir Geoffrey very shabbily, and by so doing have brought a great deal of misery upon both him and yourself."

Forgive such plainspokenness? Augusta was not one to

tolerate in others a virtue that she did not cultivate herself. "Oh!" she said faintly, and swooned gracefully across the daybed.

Tabby regarded the recumbent Lady Grey with some dismay. She was making a sad botch of this attempt at affecting a reconciliation, it seemed. Why Sir Geoffrey was so enamored of Lady Grey, Tabby could not imagine; a female of such determined refinement must find it difficult to coexist with any lesser being. But it was not Tabby's place to question her employer's choice. With a sigh, she picked up the vinaigrette and waved it beneath Lady Grey's delicate nose. This having little effect, she then tried to loosen the fastening of Augusta's yellow-spotted muslin gown.

Lady Grey regained her senses then, to realize that the female who had been before her in Sir Geoffrey's affections was now making bold with her own person in a very forward way. What *was* the creature about? It passed human bearing. "Grimsley!" Augusta wailed.

Grimsley had been hovering in the hallway, awaiting just that summons—and quite an earful she'd gotten in the meantime; there was no doubt who'd be the center of attention at the servants' table this day. She drew herself up to her full height, put on her sternest face, and went forth to evict the encroaching Mrs. Quarles.

Chapter Twelve

Vivien Sanders wore a brooding expression as he walked down the hallway of the house his sister had hired for the summer. Not all the visitors who flocked to Brighton were attracted by the salubrious waters or the bracing breezes that benefited sluggish and debilitated constitutions; nor by the possibility of viewing the remains of old Saxon camps, or royalty at play at the Pavilion, or the Tenth in review. Not that Vivien had failed to enjoy all these diversions in the past, as well as water parties and riding on the Downs, and above all the Lewes and Brighton Race Meetings, traditionally held at the end of July. But none of these attractions had lured Vivien, this time, to Brighton. And he had not, despite appearances, followed the divine Sara there. Indeed, at this particular moment, there was no thought of that lady in his mind.

The drawing room was furnished with rather rigid-looking rosewood furniture, a geometric-patterned carpet on the floor. Its effect was less to welcome than repel. As was the expression on his sister's face. "Oh, Vivien, it's only you." She had risen on his entrance and now sank back into her chair.

Here was a fine greeting from a sibling he had not spoken with in some days. Vivien frowned. "When last I saw you, you were celebrating your betrothal. Now I find you looking as though you've come from a wake. What's put you so out of humor, Gus?''

Lady Grey shuddered to hear her nickname, so recently formed on other, falser lips. "Oh, do not call me that!" she cried.

Was he never to be free of hysterical females? Vivien knew an ignoble impulse to flee. It was counterbalanced by his genuine fondness for his sister. He sighed and sat down upon a deucedly uncomfortable sofa upholstered in striped silk. "You must ask me more prettily than that!" he said in a joking tone. "In case you had failed to notice, I am grown far too large now for you to box my ears."

"Not you!" gasped Augusta. "Geoffrey!" Words failed her, and she groped for her handkerchief among the items on the small table beside her, among which Vivien counted laudanum and cordials, hartshorn and a vinaigrette. He frowned again at this indication that his sister had been doctoring herself. Although she spoke frequently of liverish depressions and oppressions on the chest, he had never taken her complaints seriously. The reek of cologne in the closed room was enough to make anyone ill, he thought. "Gus—Augusta! Are you not feeling well?" he asked.

Of course she was not feeling well. Any fool must see that. But Augusta had no wish to quarrel with her brother. "Not I!" she sniffed. "Not, that is, beyond the usual. My nerves, of course—and a certain sickness of the heart! Oh, I cannot bear to think of it!" Once more, she buried her face in her handkerchief. Her further words were muffled. Of them, Vivien understood only "Geoffrey."

Not surprisingly, Vivien deduced from this that it was not his sister, but her fiancé, who was gravely ill. "My poor Gus," he said, and offered her his handkerchief in lieu of her own. "Is it so very bad? Can nothing be done?"

Lady Grey lowered her handkerchief. There was a distinct gleam in her green eyes. "Yes! You may call him out!" she cried.

His sister wished him to call out a man who already stood at death's door? Vivien wondered if Augusta had physicked herself to the point of derangement. Or perhaps he had misunderstood her. "I thought—is not Sir Geoffrey ill?" he asked.

"Ill!" Augusta crushed the handkerchief in her fingers. "Certainly he is—of petticoat fever, it appears! I tell you, Vivien, it is very lowering to discover that one has been taken in. When I think of poor dear William—"

Vivien could not bear to hear one more paean to his deceased brother-in-law, whom he had detested in life. Since he suspected his sister's secret feelings were akin to his own, he was not gentle with her. "Poor dear William was a prig, and he did his damnedest to make you one, too! Come down off your high ropes, Gus, and tell me what all this rumption is about!"

"A prig! I am no such thing!" Lady Grey's eyes filled again with tears. "How can you be so heartless, Vivien? Just days past I was very happy—I remember it quite well! But now that wretched Quarles female has—oh, I cannot bear to think about it! Never did I think Geoffrey would use me this horrid way!"

Clearly, no neat concise explanation was to be offered. Vivien must piece together the facts. One of his sister's statements intrigued Vivien greatly. "*What* Quarles female?" he asked.

"Is there more than one?" Augusta looked dismayed. "I suppose I should not be surprised. Whoever would have thought that Geoffrey would turn out to be a philanderer, the wretch? I do not wish to be married to a philanderer, and so I have told him. One in the family is quite enough!" She glanced guiltily at Vivien. "Oh, dear! I didn't mean—"

"Don't regard it!" Vivien tried to lighten the proceed-

88

ings with his most charming smile. "I wouldn't want to be married to me, either!"

"No." Lady Grey sighed, in proof of the odd fact that sisters are immune to brotherly charms that drive other women wild. "Nor would you want to be married to Geoffrey—although I really *did*, Vivien, which is what makes it so sad. Goodness, you have never even met him, though he should have applied to you for permission to seek my hand. Yes, and I wish he had, because you would have denied it to him, because you would have recognized at once that he was a great deal too familiar with the game of hearts!"

Vivien was uncertain how it was that his sister's unhappy romance had become his fault. "You still haven't told me what happened, Gus."

"Have I not? How foolish I am being! It seems that you must already know, because it is all as clearly in my recollection as if it had happened only yesterday. Which in fact it did!" How dare Geoffrey disappoint her so? In agitation, Augusta rose from her chair and paced up and down the room. "In short, Vivien, I have learned of Geoffrey's, er, peccadilloes barely in the nick of time!"

Peccadilloes? Whatever Vivien had expected, it was not this. And what had his sister's fiancé's peccadilloes to do with his own elusive Miss Nevermind? "The deuce!" he said.

Augusta was gratified by this response. "You doubt the fidelity of your own ears!" she cried with bitter triumph. "And so did I! Or, rather, it was my eyes. You know what gentlemen are; you should not be surprised. *I* was shockingly misled. Nothing can be more revolting to propriety than to see one's fiancé's dirty linen washed in public! Unless it is one's own, of course, but I have none. And then the creature must force herself upon me against my will and tell me that I have behaved badly to Geoffrey!"

Vivien was still in the grip of a certain confusion. "You've spoken with this Quarles female?" he asked.

"Spoken with her?" echoed Lady Grey. "Indeed I have! And you need not tell me that it was a most improper thing! She wasted her breath, of course. I knew there was only one course open to me the moment that creature's existence came to light."

Vivien could not help but feel a certain sympathy for Sir Geoffrey, as well as a certain contempt for a man who so grossly mismanaged his affairs. Not that Vivien's own affairs were in excellent train at the moment. "You immediately determined to cry off."

"Of course I did!" Vivien looked stern, Augusta thought. "You must see that I have no choice! How can I remain betrothed to a man with a disagreeable stigma attached to his name? I would be plunged into the scandalbroth with him, Vivien, and I could not bear that! I know what you are thinking," she added, when his frown did not disappear. "You're thinking that your escapades should have made me more tolerant. But I know how people talk, because I spent a great many years listening to William, and I simply cannot bear to have such things said about me."

Vivien winced. He had never thought about his reputation much and had been dismayed to realize that it had caused his Miss Nevermind to run away. Now he wondered if his immense and unsought success with the ladies had caused him to grow brutish and insensitive. His elusive nemesis had also told him her name was Quarles. Now Gus told him that her betrothal was at an end due to a female named Quarles. Vivien didn't know what to think.

Augusta could not care for her brother's silence. "I cannot bear it if you should turn your face against me!" she wailed.

Vivien realized that his sister had worked herself into a

90

disturbing case of nerves. "Don't be absurd!" he said, as he took her in his arms. "Poor Gus, our chickens really have come home to roost, have they not? But you will not resolve anything by wearing a pathway in that rug! This is an awkward business, but it may not be so very bad. You are very quick to condemn your Sir Geoffrey. The truth is that you don't know what it is he has or hasn't done."

"Oh, don't I? I was not born yesterday, Vivien! Geoffrey—" Pink-cheeked, Augusta turned her face away and tried very hard not to remember how very practiced Geoffrey's kisses had been. "Were there not some truth in that woman's allegations, he would have told me about her, don't you think? But he made no effort to defend himself." She sighed. "Nor did he attempt to make a clean breast of the matter to me."

Confess all to a lady whose most likely reaction would be to send him off with a flea in his ear? Vivien considered Sir Geoffrey's failure to do so less cowardly than sensible. He also considered that his sister was making a great flap over what might be simple mischief. She was not usually so excitable. He looked searchingly down into her unhappy face. "Gus, have you been drinking?" he asked.

"Drinking! Oh!" Again, Augusta flushed. "I took some wine-and-water for my headache, if that's what you mean. Not that it has proven of the slightest benefit, so far as I can tell!"

Vivien was on the verge of developing a headache of his own. "What an excellent notion!" he said, and rang the servants' bell.

Some moments later, Mr. Sanders and his sister were again seated in the drawing room, each with a glass of the excellent claret laid down by her late spouse. "You must admit," Augusta insisted, "that Geoffrey's conduct leaves a great deal to be desired!"

Vivien considered that his sister's behavior was less than admirable. He did not say so, having no desire to engage in a brangle with her. "Shockingly irregular!" he responded lightly. "This Sir Geoffrey must surely be the greatest rascal unhanged. Cut line, Gus! I'll wager you wouldn't like your Geoffrey half so much if he hadn't blotted his copybook every now and again."

"Oh!" Augusta was aflame with embarrassment, perhaps because her brother's last remark was very near the truth. Of course Vivien would be sympathetic to Geoffrey, being himself no stranger to escapades. "But not," she said somewhat incoherently, "while he's betrothed to me!"

"But was he betrothed to you?" asked Vivien. It was not a question without merit. A man who trifled with one female while betrothed to another could well be considered a reprobate. Thought of a reprobate trifling with his sister could not please Vivien. Indeed, it made him very angry. "When did this, er, episode take place?"

Augusta recklessly drained her claret glass. "Which episode?" she asked bitterly. "Geoffrey's, er, liason with that creature? I do not know. I first became aware of her existence just yesterday. And she paid her call on me not an hour past."

Vivien began to doubt that this was the tempest in a teapot that he had first thought. Still, he was aware—none better!—of how appearances may deceive. "What does this Quarles female look like?" he asked.

Between cold fingers, Lady Grey pleated the skirt of her pretty yellow-spotted muslin gown. "Quite ordinary," she said spitefully. "Nothing out of the common way. A plump little squab of a female with nothing at all to recommend her. Except"—and her eyes filled with angry tears—"that she is quite young!"

That rankled, Vivien realized. The fact that her rival had nothing to recommend her but her youth was a blow to Gus's pride. But he required a more exact description. "What color was her hair?"

"As if I cared for such a thing!" snapped Augusta, so annoyed by her brother's question that she ceased mutilating her skirt. "What is it about that female? Now she has fascinated even you, it seems! For myself, I never heard of her before, and I wish I hadn't now!"

So did Vivien wish. Still, his sister's troubles gave him temporary respite from his own. Or might have done, if not for his suspicion that the source of their troubles was the same. "Oh, very well!" said Gus. "Her hair was brown. I already said she was quite common, so I don't know why you'd care!"

"I must know for whom I am searching," Vivien said, and rose. "You may leave Mrs. Quarles to me, Gus. I'll find out what I may about the woman, and then—well, we shall see."

Chapter Thirteen

The entire family sat down to dinner at Elphinstone House that day. Ermyntrude had dressed for the occasion in emeralds and low-cut green silk. The fare was unexceptionable: turtle soup, turbot and lobster sauce, a quarter of lamb and cauliflowers, to be followed by fruits and soft pudding, a gooseberry-and-currant pie. Cook's creations were much more conventional since Tabby had taken charge of the store cupboards and doled out weekly portions of jam and butter, sugar and tea, and cooking sherry. Even the service was unexceptionable. The food reached the table while it was still warm, and scarce a bite was spilled, a fact that warmed Tabby's weary heart and filled Lambchop—skulking in the hallway, since he was banished from the dining room—with gloom.

Tabby's heart was being wrung by the morose expression on her employer's face. She felt very culpable, as if Sir Geoffrey's predicament was some fault of hers. Tabby knew better; Sir Geoffrey's liaison with Mrs. Quarles had taken place long before Tabby arrived in Brighton. But his unhappy expression reminded Tabby of her papa, after her mama had run off. Love was a dangerous business, Tabby decided, causing people to engage in absurdly reckless acts, such as riding out on a half-broken horse. The turtle soup tasted suddenly like dishwater. Tabby set down her spoon.

Ermyntrude did likewise. She noticed that the atmosphere in the dining room was glum. It was not her fault; Ermyntrude had done her best to enliven the occasion. A pity there was none but the family to appreciate her efforts. Soon, Ermyntrude consoled herself, St. Erth would dote upon her beauty when it was presented to him in a sufficiently forceful way. Meanwhile, Ermyntrude knew that she looked her best and must content herself with that. And with the lobster sauce that she particularly liked.

But it was difficult to enjoy oneself in the midst of such gloom. Tabby was deep in a brown study, and Drusilla only nibbled at her food. Sir Geoffrey made no pretense of eating, but slumped in his chair. Ermyntrude decided that her papa was the source of the dejection that seemed to have infected them all. "Pa!" she said. "What ails you? You look quite old!"

So he looked old? Sir Geoffrey was not surprised. He supposed he'd always known that he wouldn't live to reach a ripe old age. Would Gus be sorry then for the horrid accusations she'd made to him? Remembrance of those accusations inspired Sir Geoffrey to refill his wineglass. But one could hardly discuss such things with a daughter, especially of such tender years. "Nothing!" He sighed.

Drusilla roused. She had been feeling Lambchop's absence from table very keenly and consequently had not paid her papa attention until Ermyntrude spoke. Sir Geoffrey looked even more miserable than when Lady Grey had broken off their betrothal. And he said nothing was wrong? "What a clanker!" Drusilla remarked. "You're hardly setting us a good example, Pa! I recall your saying how telling taradiddles ain't the thing."

"Did I?" Sir Geoffrey murmured vaguely. His daughters' upbringing was the least of his worries now. They'd rub on well enough without him, once he'd turned up his

95

toes. Tabby could be counted on to keep them in line. He reminded himself to amend his will so that she received a comfortable behest.

Drusilla had no patience with her papa's blue devils. "Pa!" she said again, and whacked her spoon against the table with such force that Sir Geoffrey winced. "I demand that you tell us what is plaguing you!"

Sir Geoffrey saw nothing untoward in his younger daughter's making demands of him; in his experience, making demands was what children did best of all. But he had no answers to give. "I can't explain, puss! That is, I could—I would!—but you're too young."

"There!" Ermyntrude could not deny herself a moment's triumph. "I'm sure I've said the same myself any number of times! You consider yourself quite grown-up, Dru, but the truth is that you're still a child."

"A child, am I?" Drusilla's eyes flashed. "You ain't so much older yourself. Yes, and though I may be younger, I ain't such a ninny as to make a wager I can't help but lose!"

This prediction rankled. "Never you mind my wager!" Ermyntrude snapped. "You just wish that I shall lose it, and I am determined I shall not! You'll see! I shan't dwindle into a fubsy-faced old maid! And you had best remember that it is never wise to bet against a dark horse because I have made up my mind to take the field!"

Sir Geoffrey was intrigued by this conversation. For one thing, it staggered the imagination to think that Ermyntrude might become an ape-leader. For another— "What wager?" he asked. "Gus was right; I'm a shockingly lax parent if I've failed to tell you that for young women to go about making wagers is *not* a proper thing!"

There was a brief silence at the dining table. None of Sir Geoffrey's companions wished to explain to him what the wager in question was about. "It was nothing so very bad!" Tabby said weakly. "A game—a jest!"

"Which ain't the point, anyway!" added Drusilla, before Ermyntrude could protest. "We was talking about you, Pa, and why you're in the dumps! And for you to say I'm too young to hear about it is the outside of enough. If I'm old enough to know that you've had lightskirts in your keeping, it ain't right to deprive me of the rest!"

Sir Geoffrey eyed his younger daughter in consternation. "Lightskirts?"

Drusilla shrugged impatiently. "What else would you call this Mrs. Quarles?"

Sir Geoffrey frowned, "She's not a lightskirt, puss. Merely a lady who's come down in the world. A true lightskirt is a female who"—he realized guiltily what Lady Grey would say if she could overhear him explaining the various categories of the frail but fair to his youngest child—"who was never a lady at all! It is not kind of you to speak so of Mrs. Quarles."

Ermyntrude was flushed with excitement. She had never before realized that her papa was such a profligate. "What's it like?" she asked. "To be a woman of that sort?"

Tabby was horrified by the question. "Ermyntrude!" she gasped.

Sir Geoffrey was no less dismayed and even more embarrassed. "That's a queer thing to ask," he muttered to his wineglass.

Ermyntrude didn't think her question at all strange. There were certain things she wished to know, and where better to seek an answer than from the mouth of the horse itself? "Why is it so queer?" she asked. "You should know what it's like to be a demirep since you're on such easy terms with them!"

Sir Geoffrey made haste to disabuse his daughter of this startling notion. "I'm nothing of the sort! And neither is Mrs. Quarles. We'll speak no more of this, miss!"

Ermyntrude did not care for this rebuke. "You're

mighty generous to the female who's landed you in the suds.''

Sir Geoffrey looked uncomfortable. "I was, er, fond of her once,'' he allowed. "Moreover, I'm not so sure I wouldn't have landed in the suds even without her help. The thing is, I think Gus must be mad!''

This remark caused Tabby to look up from the plate that she had been studying—a pretty thing with a lilac-pink border and gold edging, painted in the center with a poppy spray. A presentiment struck her. "Mad?'' she asked.

"Mad!'' repeated Sir Geoffrey emphatically. "Windmills in her head! Touched in the upper works. There can be no other explanation of the note she sent me, accusing me of—well!''

Sir Geoffrey's audience were on the edges of their seats. "Well?'' echoed Drusilla. "Pa, that ain't fair!''

Sir Geoffrey supposed it was not. His daughters had demonstrated themselves sufficiently worldly to hear anything he might say. "Apparently Mrs. Quarles had the temerity to call on Lady Grey, and I'm being held to blame.''

"You are being blamed?'' Drusilla echoed. "Now that *is* unfair.''

Sir Geoffrey agreed. "Not for the visit,'' he explained, "but for her age. Lady Grey has taken the notion that Mrs. Quarles is barely out of the schoolroom. *I* can only think that Gus must need spectacles, because Mrs. Quarles is forty if she's a day!'' A well-preserved forty, he recalled somewhat wistfully; but for Gus to accuse him of debauching innocents was hideously unjust. Mrs. Quarles might have been innocent in her cradle, but Sir Geoffrey would not swear even to that. "Or perhaps Gus had been unhinged by grief!'' he speculated. "Which may also be laid at my door!''

Drusilla and Ermyntrude exchanged glances, wondering if perhaps it was their papa who had become unhinged, which was certainly one explanation of his queer talk. Tabby, who knew better, returned her attention to her plate. She was stricken with guilt and cowardice and could not bring herself to confess that Lady Grey's current misapprehension was largely her fault. "And if Gus's angry now," Sir Geoffrey added, "I can't think what she'll say when she finds out that Mrs. Quarles is still living in my house!"

Living in the house? That settled it. "Pa," said Drusilla gently, "mayhap you should have a nice lie-down. When you wake up, you'll feel much better and realize there ain't no doxies—er, fallen ladies—living here with us."

Sir Geoffrey did not appreciate his daughter's solicitude. "Not here!" he snapped. "In North Street."

Ermyntrude was fascinated by these disclosures. "Pa!" she marveled. "You are in love with two females at the same time!"

Sir Geoffrey looked indignant. "I am no such thing!"

"No?" squealed Ermyntrude. "You don't love this Mrs. Quarles? Good God, Pa! If you put your mind to it, you could be quite a rake!"

Did Ermyntrude sound as though she would relish a rake for a papa? Surely not! "It was as a favor that I allowed Mrs. Quarles to borrow my house," Sir Geoffrey said. "My other house, that is. She was having financial difficulties. And then I kept expecting she would move out. One hesitated to ask, you know! But now I have had to take steps."

Drusilla couldn't imagine why Tabby was staring with such fascination at her pretty plate. Drusilla herself was much more fascinated by her papa. "I didn't know you had another house," she said.

Was Sir Geoffrey being called to account by his younger daughter? He knew he should not stand for such a thing. "Oh, I have more than one secret left!" he retorted, with a miserable attempt at jocularity. "As for the North Street house—you wouldn't like it, puss! A street steep and thick with coaching offices, abustle with traffic from dawn to dusk. It's not much of a house, anyway—which is why I never thought to mention it to you girls.''

Sir Geoffrey's girls—and Tabby—didn't believe this explanation for a moment. All three envisioned a succession of dazzling high-flyers passing through Sir Geoffrey's love nest. "I am very disappointed in Mrs. Quarles," he added. "Taking advantage of my generosity like that. And if Gus's angry now, when she finds out about the love letters, she'll be fit to skin a cat!''

Tabby broke the shocked silence. "Love letters?" she asked.

"Love letters," Sir Geoffrey repeated grimly. "There's scant hope Gus *won't* learn about them since she and Mrs. Quarles are on the way to being bosom-bows!''

"Love letters!" cried Ermyntrude. "Oh, Pa, how could you have been such a—a paper-skull? If this woman makes those letters public, we shall never live it down. And I shall never bring St. Erth to the altar, because he has a very high opinion of himself and would never stoop to associate himself with a figure of fun!''

Sir Geoffrey was uncertain how St. Erth had become involved in the conversation. Perhaps it was an indication that he had further neglected his fatherly duties. "What's this? Has St. Erth thrown the handkerchief in your direction, Ermy? If so, I suppose you may have him, though he should have asked my permission first. It's not proper that your pa be kept in perfect ignorance of what's going on, puss!''

"He hasn't popped the question yet," Ermyntrude was chagrined to admit. She shot a glance a Drusilla. "But he will!''

Tabby experienced a pang of pity for Ermyntrude. Certainly the girl was a tremendous flirt, and the incurable selfishness of her disposition was to be deplored. As for

100

this determination of hers to bring St. Erth up to scratch—well, it was patently absurd. But Tabby had her own air-dreams, and could sympathize with Ermyntrude. Tabby's memories of her own mama's disgrace were scanty, but she retained an impression of acute embarrassment and anger on her papa's part, and a distinct notion that their lives had changed dramatically from that point. Ermyntrude would not like being shunned by all her friends as result of her papa's imprudence.

But Sir Geoffrey was not the only imprudent member of the family, and Ermyntrude had made a wager that she would not wish to lose. "You might try to remember St. Erth's notion of himself," Tabby suggested. "He will want to feel similarly about the woman to whom he gives his heart."

Ermyntrude dismissed this sensible advice with a gesture. "Pooh!" said she. "That just shows all you know. St. Erth won't mind anything I do, so long as I do not make it public knowledge, so that it may be bandied about on every tongue. It is the way of the world. Not that we must blame Pa for this Quarles woman! He merely allowed his heart to rule his head, and has been shockingly taken advantage of, poor lamb!"

Sir Geoffrey appreciated this sympathy. Not that it changed anything. "Mrs. Quarles would tell you that the shoe is on the other foot. And so she may have told Gus, for all I know! One thing is certain: The cat's been set among the pigeons and is like to have a feast before it can be put back out."

Ermyntrude frowned. Her sympathy only extended so far. "I don't know how you can speak so lightly about it! Mrs. Quarles has letters of a compromising character in her possession, and she's in the process of striking up an intimate acquaintance with Lady Grey. Next thing we know, our dirty laundry will be hung out for all the world to see."

Sir Geoffrey found it very depressing to hear his love letters spoken of as dirty laundry. He took another sip of wine. Drusilla glared at her sister. "If you think St. Erth would cut up in such an event, consider Lady Grey!"

Ermyntrude did so. "Oh, poor Pa!" she cried. "I did not perfectly realize—which is not wonderful, considering all that I have on my mind—but the case is truly desperate, is it not?"

"You might say that." Sir Geoffrey slumped even more dreadfully in his chair.

Tabby roused from her own guilty reflections. "Is there nothing that may be done?"

Ermyntrude turned to her. "Of course! There generally *is* something that may be done; we need only to discover what it is!" She pushed back her chair and perambulated about the dining room, the better to facilitate her processes of thought. As she passed by the doorway, she heard Lambchop whine. Ermyntrude was not a cruel girl, for all her self-absorption. She opened the door and admitted the dog. Lambchop immediately ran under the table and flopped down across Drusilla's feet.

Tabby had not the heart to protest. What should she care, truly, if Lambchop was present in the dining room? Oh, how could Lady Grey have mistaken her for Mrs. Quarles? If the mistake were not so disastrous, it would have been absurd.

"We must visit Mrs. Quarles!" announced Ermyntrude. "And try to buy her off!"

Chapter Fourteen

And so, once more, Tabby mingled with the summer visitors to Brighton: merchants and Cyprians, sportsmen and adventurers, vacationing cits and persons of quality. She passed through streets that had known the footsteps of Burke and Fox and Sheridan; the Prince of Wales and Mrs. Fitzherbert; "Gentleman" Jackson; pale, clubfooted young Lord Byron and the slight young figure dressed in pantaloons whom he called "brother," yet who spoke in a feminine voice. Not that Tabby was especially appreciative of her surroundings as she hastened along the narrow lanes and winding streets. She was beginning to wish she had never heard the name Elphinstone and hoped this errand might be more successful than her last.

North Street was indeed a busy address, as Sir Geoffrey had said, steep and abustle with coaching inns. Tabby looked again at the address in her hand. Then she glanced up to see a carriage bearing down on her. It was a very fine cabriolet, a light conveyance with only two wheels, drawn by one horse. The passenger sat in the open and acted as his own coachman. Tabby recognized the driver. She ducked her head and stepped back a pace.

But he had seen her and drew the cabriolet to a stop. "Get in," he said.

How stern his voice was. "I cannot!" Tabby protested.

"There is something I must do, some business I must attend to!"

"I'll warrant!" retorted Mr. Sanders in tones that were sterner still. "I warn you, I will not take no for an answer. Either you enter my carriage of your own volition or I will resort to force."

Tabby blinked. The man sounded serious. And he looked serious as well. Was Tabby never to meet Mrs. Quarles? Once more fate, in the person of Vivien, had intervened.

In truth, Tabby welcomed an excuse to delay the meeting further. Perhaps in the interim she might think of what to say. "Very well," she murmured. Vivien assisted her into the cabriolet. It was no less elegant on close inspection, upholstered in crimson velvet, complete with windows and blinds. Nor was the cabriolet's owner hard to gaze upon in his long silk-lined driving coat, which was embellished with several shoulder capes and secured across the chest by a double row of mother-of-pearl buttons. His white-topped boots were as excellently made as his high-crowned beaver hat and his York-tan gloves. But he was glowering at her in such a dreadful manner. Tabby sought for a light tone of voice. "What did you wish to speak to me about? It must be dreadfully important—or perhaps you are in the habit of abducting females, sir?"

It wasn't his own habits that concerned Vivien at this moment, or his character. "How *could* you involve yourself with a cursed rum touch like Elphinstone?"

Tabby flushed at the realization that Vivien had found her out. No wonder he looked angry. Mr. Sanders would consider it beneath his dignity to flirt with a mere governess. "I had no choice," she said quietly. "And you should not speak so unkindly of Sir Geoffrey. He has been very good to me."

"Good?" echoed Vivien in disbelief. "At least no one may say you are disloyal! But, my God! Why him?"

Tabby could not imagine why Vivien had taken such a dislike to her employer. "I had no choice!" she replied. "No one else offered me a place, even though I advertised. Believe me, I was very grateful when Sir Geoffrey's man of business contacted me."

The matter had been arranged by Sir Geoffrey's man of business? The wench had *advertised*? Involved though he may have been in various escapades and scandals, Vivien had never heard of such a thing. So stunned was he by his companion's disclosures that he failed to pay attention to the street. Consequently, some moments were spent extricating himself from a traffic jam. Once that was accomplished, he prudently turned onto a quieter road that led out of town. "Elphinstone," he said grimly, "has much to answer for!"

Tabby could not care for Vivien's tone of voice or for his angry expression. "If not Sir Geoffrey, it would have been someone else. My position could be a great deal worse! I wish you would tell me what is bothering you," she added. "Because your ill temper is spoiling what I might otherwise have enjoyed very well! Since you know the truth, I needn't pretend to you that carriage rides like this often come my way."

How frankly she spoke of her detour from the straight and narrow path. Most of the high-flyers of Vivien's acquaintance were not so candid. Not that his companion was remotely like any high-flyer Vivien had ever known. And why should she consider a carriage ride such a treat? Elphinstone was sufficiently plump in the pocket to own any number of carriages of his own. It was a strange man who would refuse to take his *petite amie* for an outing. "Elphinstone didn't take you out driving?" Vivien inquired.

"Why, no, why should he?" Tabby thought Vivien certainly had an odd notion of a governess's life. "But you still haven't told me what you wished to speak to me about!''

"Ah, but I have." For reasons he could not explain even to himself, Vivien was very angry at this point. "Let us put our cards on the table—Mrs. Quarles!''

"Mrs.—'' Why should he call her that? Tabby remembered the gala when Vivien demanded she give him a name. "Oh! There's been a mistake. I'm not—''

"I know exactly what you are!" snapped Vivien. In truth, his ill temper was due in some part to the knowledge that he had not been the one to introduce his companion to the fleshpots. "No wonder you seemed afraid of me. You were afraid I'd tumble to your little game!''

Tabby was bewildered. "Game?'' she echoed.

They had passed beyond the outskirts of town, and Vivien drew up his horse. "You needn't try to pull the wool over my eyes; it won't work! It's not Lady Grey you're dealing with now. You may be frank with me, my dear. How much will it take to buy you off?''

"You are acquainted with Lady Grey?" Tabby was relieved to have some light shed on the mystery. Lady Grey, she remembered, had had much to say regarding depravity and vice. "No wonder you think ill of me! But it was a misunderstanding. Pray allow me to explain!''

Vivien turned to Tabby, grasped her shoulders. He didn't know if he wished more to make love to her or to give her a good shake. "I said before that I'm not a flat, my dear! You may spare me your further Banbury tales.''

Tabby was horrified that he should think so ill of her. ''But—''

"You mismanaged the business badly, did you not?'' Vivien interrupted. "Lady Grey has cried off already, and nothing Elphinstone may do will cause her to change her mind.''

Tabby was growing angry in her own turn, though not due to Vivien's opinion of Mrs. Quarles, which might well have been true. "You are eager to condemn your fellow man!" she cried. "That, sir, is very much like the pot calling the kettle black! *You* are a self-admitted rakehell, while Sir Geoffrey is a good and honorable gentleman whom Lady Grey has treated shabbily."

Vivien did not care for this allegation. "We will leave my affairs out of this!" he snapped.

Tabby had no wish to discuss Mr. Sanders's affairs until he forbade her to do so. "No!" she retorted immediately then, "we shall not! You condemn Sir Geoffrey for a past liaison while you flirt with other women practically under your mistress's nose! It seems to me that you are hardly qualified to judge any one else's conduct, sir!"

Vivien had the grace to flush. "You don't understand," he said, somewhat feebly.

Tabby opened her eyes wide. "Then perhaps you might be good enough to enlighten me as to the difference!"

Vivien would have liked to do so. He was sure there must be a difference between himself and Sir Geoffrey, but he couldn't think offhand what it might be. His thoughts were in a muddle, due to his very confused emotions concerning the female whose shoulders he still clutched. Moreover, he'd just realized that did she make this business with Sir Geoffrey public, it might give the divine Sara—as well as a number of other females of his acquaintance—some very unpleasant ideas.

"Let us speak without roundaboutness!" he said roughly. "How much do you want?"

So they were back to that. Tabby shook her head. "I don't know what you mean."

Vivien's hands tightened. "Perhaps Augusta has played right into your hands."

"Augusta?" Here was an unexpected intimacy. It seemed that Mr. Sanders and Sir Geoffrey's bride-to-be were on very close terms. Tabby wondered now just who had played whom false. "Good God, is not Sara enough for you?" she gasped.

Obviously the divine Sara was not enough for Vivien, or he would not have currently been suffering torments on this devious creature's behalf. He was not inclined to explain the matter in that light. "Don't try to change the subject!" he retorted. "Let us call a spade by its proper name, if you please!"

Tabby was ordinarily a devotee of plainspokenness, but this situation called for a degree of tact. That gentlemen amused themselves with pretty actresses and opera dancers was a fact of life that Tabby could accept. But for the same gentlemen to go about seducing ladies of quality who were affianced to other gentlemen—well, Tabby was not so broad-minded as that. "How could you!" she cried. "Perry did not tell me the half of it when he warned me about you. He should have told me that you are the greatest blackguard alive!"

Vivien was uncertain how he had become the villain of the piece. *"I?"*

"You!" Tabby blinked back angry tears. "If you were not intimately acquainted with Lady Grey, she would not have confided in you. She must trust you very much, I think. Certainly more than she trusts Sir Geoffrey. And she dared call *me* depraved! You told me you had to live up to your wicked reputation, but this goes beyond the limits of being acceptable!"

So it did. His companion thought he had seduced Gus? Vivien was shocked by the extent of the misdeed of which he had been accused. "The devil!" he said, and released Tabby. "Even I am not so wicked as *that*."

Tabby was bewildered by his horrified expression. Absurdly, she wished to offer him comfort. "I suppose there is not a great deal of difference between Lady Grey and Sara," she offered. "Save that Lady Grey is a lady of quality who is—was—betrothed to someone else."

108

Vivien frowned. "Can it be you do not know that Lady Grey is my sister?" he asked.

"Your sister!" echoed Tabby. "Oh! I thought—"

Vivien could not help but be amused by her embarrassment. "You thought that even Gus had fallen victim to my wicked charm. And I thought that you were accusing me of leading my own sister up the primrose path. So we both were mistaken, were we not?"

So they had been. So, for that matter, Vivien still was. His smile, at such close range, was dizzying. "I suppose I should not be surprised that Lady Grey is your sister," Tabby murmured. "There is a certain rigidity in both of you, a conviction that your understanding could not be at fault."

This blunt statement recalled Vivien to the purpose of this encounter. His smile faded. He was very disappointed that his Miss Nevermind should stoop so low as to try to blackmail his sister and very angry with himself for wanting her all the same. "You still have not told me your price."

Tabby had not told Vivien a number of things. He would not believe her if she sought to do so now. "I don't suppose it would do any good to ask you to trust me." She sighed.

Trust her? Vivien was not so foolish. In fact, he wondered now if he had not already trusted her too well. "How cleverly you contrived to whet my interest," he said bitterly. "You will laugh when I tell you I've scoured this accursed city for you, but to no avail—I could not find out where you lived, even when I had your name! I suppose you wanted a second string to your bow, in case Elphinstone refused to come up to scratch. You bungled badly, didn't you? Don't try to convince me that you had no idea other than revenge!"

Tabby was growing very tired of these accusations. "So now Sir Geoffrey is no longer a cursed rum touch, but I am, instead? Did I think you'd listen, I might try to change your mind—but the effort would obviously be a waste of my time!''

Despite himself, Vivien could not help but appreciate this display of temper and the way his companion's brown eyes flashed. "Try me," he said, and caught her wrist.

Tabby thought she would not. Let Vivien think her a blackmailing hussy. What difference did it make? He had no real feeling for her, or he could not have accused her of the things he had. "Sir Geoffrey is an honorable gentleman," she repeated wearily. "He means your sister no harm. As for myself, I did not contrive to meet you, but I do not expect you to believe that."

Vivien wished very much to believe her; and he wished as well not to be made a fool a second time. There was one way he knew to test a female's true feelings. "What a coil this is!" he groaned, and drew Tabby into his arms.

It was a lovely kiss. The second was no less excellent, nor was the third. Lest matters grow entirely out of hand— they were in an open carriage, after all, on a public if little-used road—Vivien drew back. "Stop this nonsensical business and let me take care of you!" he said.

Tabby's emotions were truly in a turmoil now. So well had she enjoyed Vivien's embraces that she had briefly forgotten he believed her to be a demirep. Consequently, his offer made her furious, both with him and with herself.

Vivien mistook her silence for calculation. He could not blame her for weighing the advantages of the alliance he had offered her, he supposed. Or was she still thinking of Elphinstone? "You *are* free of all, er, previous entanglements, are you not?" he inquired delicately.

Tabby's temper was mounting. "*I* am!" she retorted. "But I believe that *you* are not!"

Somewhat belatedly, Vivien recalled the divine Sara. "That needn't concern you!" he replied. "Truth be told, I should have broken it off weeks ago." He touched Tabby's cheek. "Do you wish, you shall make me heart-whole in an instant," he murmured. "You shall have your own house and as many carriage rides as you desire. Indeed, you shall have a carriage of your own! I mean to set you up in the best possible style."

"Certainly you do!" retorted Tabby. "You are a man of substance, after all, a well-breeched swell! And one who is incorrigibly fond of the ladies, as well. Do you make the same promises to all of them? When you are desirous of mounting a mistress, you will promise anything?"

Vivien flushed at this plainspokenness. Clearly his companion was angry. He was unsure what he'd done to offend. But he knew one way to stop her from talking such fustian. He reached for her again.

This time, however, Tabby was on guard. She boxed Vivien's ears. While he was still cursing, she climbed awkwardly down from the carriage and set out across the hilly downs toward Brighton.

Chapter Fifteen

The hour was considerably advanced when Tabby limped up the steps of Elphinstone House, and her anger was largely dissipated by that time. She regretted her display of temper. Even though Vivien might have refused to listen, she wished she had attempted to explain. Now she would never know how Vivien might have reacted, whether he would have been sympathetic to her tale or whether he would have scoffed. No further opportunity for explanations would present itself, she knew. Vivien was clearly furious. Had he followed her, offered her a ride back to Brighton in his cabriolet, Tabby would not have refused. But he had driven off in the opposite direction without another word.

It was for the best, Tabby told herself, as she crept quietly up the stairs. Mr. Sanders thought her a woman of very low condition, after all. He would hardly have offered to set her up as his mistress otherwise. Tabby was not shocked by the suggestion, indeed half wished that she might fling her bonnet over the windmill as he asked. There was more of her mother in her than Tabby had previously realized.

But to follow in her mama's footsteps was unthinkable, would deny her uncle's many kindnesses, perhaps even her papa's untimely death. She was doomed to be conventional and upright. On this gloomy reflection, Tabby walked into her room. She was glad no one had seen her enter the house. Tabby wanted nothing more just then than to be left alone to enjoy a good cry. She closed the door behind her and prepared to fling herself upon the bed. Then she espied an envelope propped up on her pillow. Scrawled across it was her name.

Tabby recognized Ermyntrude's handwriting. Frowning, she opened the note. Ermyntrude's handwriting was very precise, but her spelling was wildly original. It took Tabby several moments to understand that Ermyntrude was preparing to elope.

An elopement! Tabby sank down on the bed. Just when she'd thought that everything was going as badly as possible, matters rapidly became worse. Tabby was tempted to let the silly chit perish in her own intrigues. One might think it spring, there was so much romantic nonsense in the air. But Tabby couldn't let Ermyntrude make the error that she must guard against herself. Though an elopement might result in a legal union, it was almost as scandalous as if not. Warily, Tabby set out in search of Drusilla. It was bad enough that she must struggle with her own conscience without acting as Ermyntrude's as well.

Drusilla was in her papa's study, pouring over a medical book—reading about brain fever in an attempt to understand her parent. She was glad to be interrupted and greeted Tabby with a relief that was short-lived. Perhaps Drusilla was being overly influenced by her choice of reading matter, but it seemed to her that there was an unstable quality to Tabby's voice, a certain manic glitter in her eye. As for what she had to say, that was even queerer. "What do you want with Osbert?" Drusilla asked.

"Never mind that!" retorted Tabby. Time was of the essence if Ermyntrude's elopement was to be aborted. Perhaps she was already too late. "Answer me, Dru!"

113

Drusilla had just read that it was unwise to argue with a deranged person. "His home is on the Royal Crescent. I told you he is very rich."

Tabby almost groaned. Of course, Mr. Philpotts could not reside just around the corner, but must dwell on the city's outskirts. Tabby thought of her sore feet. Again she was tempted to abandon Ermyntrude to her fate. Again she could not do so. "Have you any money?" she asked Drusilla, for Sir Geoffrey's troubles had made him remiss about paying her her wage. "I must hire a hack."

A hack? Indeed, this was madness. Furthermore, Drusilla had no funds to lend, but to thwart a person in the grip of a brain fever might well result in a paroxysm of madness. "Take Pa's rig!" Drusilla suggested. "He won't care. I'll send word to the stable myself!"

So she did, as well as instructions to the coachman to keep a close eye on his passenger. Fortunately unaware of these latter instructions, Tabby set out in search of Mr. Philpotts. Perhaps it was unwise to involve an outsider in Ermyntrude's escapade, but Tabby could not deal with the situation without help. She dared not apprise Sir Geoffrey of his daughter's fit of folly, and Drusilla was too young to be of any real assistance. Tabby could only hope that Mr. Philpotts's obvious feelings for Ermyntrude would make him discreet.

The Royal Crescent—fourteen houses built by a local architect at the expense of an Indiana nabob—had only recently risen on the seafront. Although the bow fronts didn't meet with universal approval, lodgings there were sought by the most distinguished of company. Tabby didn't wait for the coachman's assistance but climbed down quickly from the carriage and hastened to the front door of Mr. Philpotts's residence.

A young footman answered her summons. "The master is not to home," he said in dignified accents.

"Oh, no!" gasped Tabby. "Do you know where I may

114

find him? It is most important—a matter of life and death!''

The footman had not been long at his post. Even so, he should have known better than to make free of his master's whereabouts to every person who came knocking at the door. But this person was of the female gender, and the footman was so startled by her appearance that he spoke before he thought, and allowed that he believed Mr. Philpotts might have adjourned with friends to the Castle Tavern. Tabby thanked the man and hurried back to the carriage. The coachman was startled to receive her next directions. Still, Miss Drusilla had said only to keep an eye on his passenger, not to refuse to do her bidding, and so he obeyed her queer command.

Mr. Philpotts was indeed at the Castle Tavern, enjoying some pleasant conversation and some excellent ale. The talk was all of the races that would soon take place. The best horses were brought from Newmarket and the North to run in the Brighton and Lewes Races, and immense sums of money were wagered on the outcome. Mr. Philpotts was deep in an intense conversation concerning the noblest friend of man—to be precise, the rival virtues of two specimens thereof known respectively as Jack Come Tickle Me and Kiss in a Corner—and was not pleased to be interrupted before his point had been made. But when he learned that the person so insistent of speaking with him was a female, he abruptly left the room.

Tabby was waiting in the hallway. Her appearance there was so unexpected that Mr. Philpotts stopped dead in his tracks. Of course, it had been foolish to hope that Ermyntrude would burst into the tavern and demand to see him. ''Miss Minchin, you should not be here! Is anything amiss?''

''Naturally something is amiss!'' retorted Tabby. Her rudeness may perhaps be forgiven her in light of the fact

115

that she was having an absolutely wretched day. "We cannot talk here! Pray come with me, sir."

Mr. Philpotts was not of an adventurous nature. Ordinarily, he would have been startled to receive such an invitation from a scarce-known female. On this occasion, however, he had a rather nasty presentiment and therefore followed Tabby with reluctance. "It's Ermy, isn't it?" he asked, when they arrived in the street.

Tabby paused. She was taking a great risk in trusting this seemingly pleasant young man. "Forgive me, but there is a good reason for my question. You care a great deal for Ermyntrude, do you not?"

Mr. Philpotts's presentiment worsened. "I would go to the devil for her," he said.

Tabby sought to ignore the ignoble pang of envy that struck her at these words. "Then I must trust you!" She handed Osbert Ermyntrude's note.

He frowned at it, then turned pale. "You came here to tell me that Ermy has set out to make herself a viscountess? I'd much rather you had not!" he remarked. "I knew that she had a preference for St. Erth; everyone did! But I did not realize that *he*—"

"He doesn't! interrupted Tabby. "At least that anyone has seen. I believe that this so-called elopement is something that Ermy has dreamed up without any encouragement from St. Erth. We are wasting time, Mr. Philpotts! You must help me prevent Ermy from landing herself in the scandal-broth—if it is not already too late!"

Mr. Philpotts had suffered a severe blow and still was not reasoning clearly. "I don't see what we can do. Ermy must be allowed to make her own choice."

"Ermyntrude," Tabby said bluntly, "is a fine vulgar miss who can be trusted only to indulge herself in some shockingly irregular misconduct! And what you may do, sir—if possible—is help me prevent her going from bad to worse. We are not accomplishing anything standing here

116

like this. If you will not come with me, then at least tell me St. Erth's address!"

Mr. Philpotts had meant to explain to Miss Minchin that he would not be so presumptuous as to condemn Ermyntrude for her conduct, no matter how miserable he might be made as a result of it. Upon hearing her words, he looked rather astonished instead. "*You* mean to call on St. Erth?" he asked.

"I mean to do something!" cried Tabby. "If you will not help me, then I must myself somehow contrive to extricate Ermyntrude from her foolishness. Good day, Mr. Philpotts! Pray forgive me for taking you away from your friends." She turned toward the waiting carriage.

Her scornful words stung. Osbert realized he had not acquitted himself well. He realized also that he could not in good conscience allow Miss Minchin to set out unaccompanied to the rescue. Ermyntrude must be more important to him than the outcome of a horse race, after all. Even if she was in the process of eloping with someone else. "Miss Minchin, wait! I wish to accompany you!" He hurried after her, gave the coachman an address.

The carriage clattered through the streets. "Perhaps it's all a hum," ventured Mr. Philpotts. "Ermy's so high-spirited, she might have done it for a lark."

"No," Tabby responded unsympathetically, "she did it to win a wager. Damned imprudent is what she is, sir! I only hope we are not too late to save her from the consequences of her foolishness. Thank God! Here is the hotel."

A brief argument ensued. Mr. Philpotts thought he should be the one to confront the viscount, and Tabby had no intention that the confrontation should take place without her there. In the end, they both entered the hotel. "Wager?" Osbert inquired.

"It was nothing!" Tabby responded tersely. "A bargain with her sister concerning the disposition of their grand-

117

mama's pearls. We have no time to stand here gossiping, Mr. Philpotts! You must take me to St. Erth.''

Looks were definitely deceiving, decided Osbert; no one would guess at first glance that Miss Minchin should be such a gorgon. She put him strongly in mind of a governess of his own, who had more than once made him wish to run away. Not that he could blame Miss Minchin for Ermyntrude's elopement or for her current distress. Osbert had wished himself, sometimes, that Ermyntrude would refrain from rushing into certain trouble, and he wished now that he was not such a dull stick as to preclude her ever thinking of involving him in her escapades. He could not help but admire her reckless daring. Without another word of argument, he escorted Tabby to the rooms hired for the summer by Viscount St. Erth.

The viscount was in. He had not planned to be, had been engaged with friends for a gentlemen's whist party, to be followed by a little music and a cold chicken and some sandwiches afterward. However, fate had contrived that he should pass his time otherwise. This circumstance annoyed him greatly. It was with a savage expression that he flung open his door. ''Hah!'' he said. *''Hah!* I had expected you sooner—not that it would have accomplished you anything! I'm no pigeon for anybody's plucking, and so I told that damned little minx, and so I will also tell you!''

Mr. Philpotts did not care to hear Ermyntrude spoken of a minx. He would have stepped forward had not Tabby taken firm hold of his coat sleeve. ''Wait!'' she hissed. ''Sir, am I to take it that Ermyntrude has been here?''

''Been here?'' echoed the viscount. ''I should say she has. She gained entry by disguising herself as a page. But you already know that! Why else should *you* be here? You were to burst in and find us in a compromising position, and then I would be honor bound to do the proper thing! Don't bother to deny it; the chit confessed as much!'' His handsome face was almost feral. "I had my man take her home. So now you may leave also, because you are too late!" Without waiting for a response, he closed the door in Tabby's face.

She deemed it safe, now, to release Mr. Philpotts's sleeve. "What a wretched child she is!" Tabby sighed. "I suppose we must be glad that she is safe. I shall have a few words to say to her, I promise you, sir. I know that I may trust you to say nothing of this. I only hope St. Erth will be as closemouthed."

"He will." Osbert accompanied Tabby to her carriage. "He wouldn't want his part in it to become known. The thing is, Miss Minchin, if it does—well, you're in a bit of a spot yourself. You shouldn't have come to the Castle looking for me, and you shouldn't have been in St. Erth's rooms."

This observation struck Tabby as the height of absurdity. But it would be unkind to scoff at Mr. Philpotts, especially after she had taken him from his friends to accompany her on a wild-goose chase. "I wasn't in his rooms, but in the hallway!" she pointed out. "And it is Ermyntrude's good name that we are concerned about, not mine."

Osbert didn't wish to think of Ermyntrude's good name, which she had tried so hard to cast away. "Ermy," he retorted, "at least had the foresight to put on a disguise so no one would know her if she was seen. You made no attempt to disguise yourself, Miss Minchin. It could be very embarrassing if you were recognized."

Embarrassing for whom? Tabby wondered if Mr. Philpotts's concern was for her own reputation or for his own. Then she thought that she misjudged him. Mr. Philpotts was not one to put selfish considerations first.

Tabby held out of hand. "You have been very good," she said. "Thank you for accompanying me. I should not have asked you—but we had no way of knowing things

119

would work out as they have. May I return you to your tavern? No? I must go home now and read Ermyntrude a dreadful scold, and so I will say good-bye!''

Osbert had taken Tabby's proffered hand. Now he released it. "I wish you would not," he said. "You will just make her even more contrary by putting obstacles in her road.''

Tabby thought Mr. Philpotts seemed to understand Ermyntrude very well. It was a pity Ermyntrude's wager didn't concern him rather than St. Erth. Although Tabby couldn't imagine Osbert lending himself to an elopement. He helped her into the carriage. "Good day!" she said to him, and to the coachman, "Elphinstone House!"

Chapter Sixteen

Despite Mr. Philpotts's advice to the contrary, Tabby had every intention of reading Ermyntrude a tremendous scold. She rehearsed her speech on the way back to Elphinstone House. If Ermyntrude uttered one objectionable word, Tabby would shake her till the teeth rattled in her head. In Tabby's opinion, Sir Geoffrey's elder daughter would benefit greatly from being turned across someone's knee and having her backside warmed with a hairbrush. Tabby regretted that she could not presume to take such direct action. St. Erth had said he sent Ermyntrude home. She hoped Ermyntrude had stayed there. Tabby dismissed the coachman and entered Elphinstone House.

The house was very quiet. Tabby was uneasy when no footman met her at the door. Had some fresh disaster taken place in her absence? She hurried down the hallway, in search of some member of the family. Then she espied the footman outside the drawing room. He had a fascinated expression on his face, and his ear pressed to the closed door.

Tabby cleared her throat. The footman jumped and looked guilty. Tabby brushed aside his explanations, watched him retreat along the hallway out of sight. Then she squared her shoulders and knocked on the drawing room door.

The entire family was within. Ermyntrude, still in page's attire, sprawled rebelliously on the window seat. Sir Geoffrey leaned against the marble mantlepiece, his head in his hands. Lambchop and Drusilla shared the zebrawood sofa. "There you are!" said the latter on Tabby's entrance. "We was wondering where you'd got to. Just wait until you hear what Ermy's done now!"

Tabby glanced back down the hallway to make sure no servants hovered within earshot, then firmly closed the door. "I know what Ermyntrude has done!" she said grimly. "She left me a note; I set out to prevent her making a byword of herself—and consequently had a most illuminating conversation with St. Erth!"

Ermyntrude still thought her scheme had been a nacky one, and the fact that it had gone awry made her cross as crabs. "Everything would be on the road to being settled by now," she said sulkily, "if you had not been so late!"

"I?" Tabby sank down on a rosewood chair. "You *were* counting on me to come after you! I thought St. Erth had misunderstood something you had said. Oh, Ermyntrude, how could you be such a—"

"Pea-brain?" supplied Drusilla. "Goose-cap?"

Ermyntrude ignored her younger sister. "What did St. Erth say?" she asked eagerly of Tabby. "The fact that he had his man accompany me home argues a degree of interest, don't you think? He could have just turned me out!"

Tabby marveled at Ermyntrude's ability to interpret a situation in the way that best suited her. "He said that you are a damned little minx, and I could not disagree! Although I thought Mr. Philpotts would offer him some violence."

"Mr. Philpotts?" In her surprise, Ermyntrude sat up straight. "You told *Osbert*? How could you!"

"How could I set off to rescue you," Tabby countered, "when I hadn't the slightest notion where to go? I thought

122

you didn't care a button for Mr. Philpotts—though I'll be hanged if I understand why you don't prefer him to St. Erth! Mr. Philpotts is all kindness and consideration, and rich as the devil as well. But that's past praying for! For you to discover in yourself a fondness for so unexceptionable a gentleman would be unthinkable. Instead, you must do your damnedest to sink yourself below reproach. You are very lucky that things worked out as they did, Ermyntrude, else your reputation would be in shreds!''

Ermyntrude was made even more cross by this tongue-lashing. ''I'd rather be thought bachelor's fare than an old cat!'' she snapped. Tabby flushed, and Ermyntrude immediately felt guilty. ''Oh, Tabby, truly I did not mean that! It's just that everyone is angry, and now you are ringing a regular peal over me, and all I wished to do was bring St. Erth up to scratch before word of Pa's love letters got out and threw a rub in my way!''

Tabby thought Ermyntrude had thrown a rub in her own way. St. Erth would avoid her like the plague now that he knew he was marked down as her victim. Tabby realized that Ermyntrude's cheeks were tear-streaked and felt reluctant pity for the girl. No doubt Sir Geoffrey had already scolded her. Tabby would say no more.

Sir Geoffrey raised his head from his hands. His handsome cheeks were pale. ''It is I who must come under the gravest censure, not Ermyntrude,'' he said. ''None of this would have occurred were I not such a miserable failure as a parent.''

''Oh, Pa, cut line!'' Drusilla said quickly, before he could again indulge in painful self-recrimination and Ermyntrude again dissolve into guilty tears. ''It wasn't you as dressed up Ermy like a page and sent her after St. Erth! Indeed, you would've forbade her to do it if she'd asked, and that she didn't ask is because she's a pea-goose, and that ain't to be laid at your doorstep!''

Sir Geoffrey looked doubtfully at his younger daughter. "It's not?"

Drusilla shook her head. "No. She's been like that as long as I've known her. I suspect she was born that way! But here's Tabby come to tell us how she spoke with Mrs. Quarles!"

How Tabby hated to be the bearer of further bad tidings. "I wish I could tell you that I convinced Mrs. Quarles to be reasonable, but the truth of the matter is that I didn't speak to her at all." She sighed. "I meant to, certainly, but—I shall try another day!"

Sir Geoffrey looked even more unhappy. "I guess I was mistaken in you, too!" He sighed. "I made sure you were sent especially to help us in our time of need. I thought you would *wish* to help us, being as we have treated you as one of the family. Not that I mean to scold you, puss! I'm sure you've done your best. I expect our troubles are too much for an outsider to bear."

Tabby wished, as Ermyntrude had before her, that Sir Geoffrey had seen fit to read her a scold. She felt very guilty that he should take the responsibility for her failure upon himself. Consequently, she said something she might ordinarily have not. "You did not tell me Lady Grey had a brother, sir!"

So Sir Geoffrey had not. Indeed the matter had quite slipped his mind. "Forgot about it!" he admitted. "Never met the fellow myself. Gus quite dotes on him, I gather, though he's a bit of a scamp—but so what if she does?"

Everyone doted on Mr. Sanders, thought Tabby. With the exception of herself. "The thing is, I know him, sir! That is, he doesn't know who I am—oh, dear! I suppose I should explain."

Sir Geoffrey allowed as he thought this might be helpful. Tabby began at the beginning of her odd acquaintance with Vivien. She told of her arrival at the inn and Perry's generous offer of a room, of Vivien's subsequent visit, and of even the divine Sara's hysteria. Sir Geoffrey looked startled, and Ermyntrude envious. "And then, at the theater, I encountered him again," Tabby continued, "when I set out looking for Ermyntrude and Mr. Philpotts. And he was at the party when I went to look for Mrs. Quarles."

"Aha!" crowed Ermyntrude. "I knew you had an assignation with someone when you filched my dress!"

"I did not!" Tabby retorted crossly. "I didn't wish to wear your dress, and I didn't wish to encounter Vivien! Er, Mr. Sanders, that is! But I did, and he wouldn't let me go until I told him my name. I didn't wish to tell him the truth, and so I said I was Mrs. Quarles."

Sir Geoffrey was trying very hard to make sense of this narration. "Oh!" he said encouragingly.

"And then," continued Tabby, "I met him again today in North Street. He insisted on taking me up in his carriage."

Ermyntrude's interest was also whetted. "Was it a very fine carriage?" she asked enviously. "What does he look like?"

"Yes, it is very fine," said Tabby. "A cabriolet. And Mr. Sanders is also very fine, and very wicked. He is Miss Divine's, er, special friend. So you may be sure she will have little to say to St. Erth."

Ermyntrude could not like this choice of words. "St. Erth is not on the dangle for that female! And if he was, no gentleman alive could hold a candle to him!"

Tabby did not care to argue the respective virtues—or vices—of Mr. Sanders and Viscount St. Erth. Better Ermyntrude's interest should remain fixed on the viscount than that Vivien should catch her eye. "*Why* did he take you up in his carriage?" Ermyntrude persisted. "You were supposed to be bargaining with Mrs. Quarles, Tabby, not enjoying a carriage ride!"

Sir Geoffrey thought his elder daughter was being a trifle harsh. "There, there, Ermy!" he said. "I'm sure Tabby is entitled to have a little fun!"

"You misunderstand," Tabby protested. "Mr. Sanders did not wish to take me on a pleasure ride."

Sir Geoffrey frowned. This tale could be better told, he thought. "Then what *did* he want?"

What Vivien had wished to offer Tabby was a slip on the shoulder. She twisted her fingers in her lap. "Apparently he had just spoken with Lady Grey. He wished to tell me that I am depraved, Sir Geoffrey, and that you are even worse. Mr. Sanders has taken the notion that you, er, led me up the primrose path."

"The primrose path?" Sir Geoffrey was dumbfounded. "That settles it. Gus *has* run mad! Where does she get these queer notions? First Mrs. Quarles, now this!"

Tabby took a deep breath. Confession, she told herself, was good for the soul. "I'm afraid," she murmured, "that Lady Grey thinks I *am* Mrs. Quarles. I went to speak with her *about* Mrs. Quarles, but apparently her footman mixed the message up. By the time I realized what had happened, she had fainted, and there was no reasoning with her after that."

Sir Geoffrey as so stunned by these disclosures that he abandoned the mantelpiece for a chair. "Fainted? Gus fainted?" he echoed.

"Yes, but I don't think you need worry about her health," Tabby responded wryly. "She was quite vigorous in her denunciations once she recovered her wits."

Sir Geoffrey was feeling anything but vigorous himself. "So that's why she accused me of snatching innocents from the cradle!" he sighed. "Well, that's one mystery cleared up!"

Tabby felt no better for her confession. Indeed, Sir Geoffrey's woebegone expression only intensified her guilt. "I am so very sorry!" she said, on the verge of tears. "I truly wished to help."

Of course she had, and was obviously feeling her failure very keenly. Sir Geoffrey had endured enough suffering of late that he didn't wish to intensify anyone else's misery. "You did your best!" he said kindly. "It's not your fault that it all went awry.

"I'm not so sure," said Tabby, deep in gloom. "If I hadn't meddled, at least Lady Grey would not think I was Mrs. Quarles!"

Drusilla released Lampchop, to that animal's great relief, because she had been hugging him all this while. Before further unpleasant events could cause her to clutch at him again, he took refuge beneath the window seat. Drusilla paid scant heed to her pet's defection. Her relief at having Tabby's earlier queer behavior explained had not been long-lived. Chasing after Ermyntrude in an attempt to prevent a disastrous elopement was commendable behavior. Rubbing elbows with a rakehell was quite another thing. It was perfectly clear to Drusilla that Mr. Sanders was a rakehell. "I had hoped for better from you, Tabby!" she said in disgust. "You're as bad as Pa or Ermy! Falling in love with Lady Grey's brother, who thinks you're his sister's fiancé's ladybird!"

"Hang it!" cried Tabby crossly. "I am *not* in love with him. How could I be? I am just a governess, if you will recall!"

The Elphinstones exchanged glances. None was so unkind as to comment on the fact that their governess was obviously given, at least in this instance, to uttering untruths. Of course she was in love with Mr. Sanders. And that, under the circumstances, was very sad.

"And even if I was, it would do me little good," Tabby continued somberly; having started her confession, she found she could not stop. "For he has made it very clear what sort of female he thinks me to be!"

"Oh!" cried Ermyntrude. This was better than the ro-

127

mance novels to which she was addicted. "What did he *do*?"

Tabby's cheeks were rosy. "He offered to buy me off. He wished to know my price." Her voice trembled. "He offered to set me up in my own little house!"

"He didn't!" Ermyntrude's eyes were big as saucers. "What did you say?"

Tabby studied her hands. "I boxed his ears. And then I walked back home and found that you had eloped, and here we are."

It seemed to Ermyntrude that Tabby's adventures made her own seem insignificant in comparison, and she thought this unfair. However, she knew how Tabby must be feeling—had not Ermyntrude had her own recent experience with as-yet-unrequited love? She left the window seat and went to perch on the arm of Tabby's chair. "Never mind!" she said kindly as she patted Tabby's shoulder. "It will all work out for the best; you'll see!"

Tabby's confessions had left her exhausted and ashamed of her outburst. "It doesn't matter," she said quietly. "I do not expect that I shall encounter Mr. Sanders again—indeed, I mean to avoid him at all costs!" She had a sudden vision of herself and Viscount St. Erth skulking about Brighton in an attempt to avoid those members of the opposite sex who plotted their ruin. The image was so absurd that she had to smile.

That smile relieved Drusilla. She wasn't certain, but she thought people who could smile hadn't gone completely round the bend. She cast an anxious glance at her papa, who had reverted to his earlier posture, head clasped in his hands. "Well, there's no denying we're in a muddle!" she said briskly. "But even muddles can be undone. It seems to me we'd do better to plan our strategy than to cry over spilled milk!"

Ermyntrude had recovered from her earlier disappointment, at least sufficiently that she wasn't going to be dictated to by her younger sister. "We've already made plans!" she said. "Weren't you paying attention, Dru?"

Drusilla had been paying very close attention. In all the disclosures of the past hour, she had not heard one constructive suggestion made. "*What* plan?" she asked suspiciously.

Ermyntrude surveyed one outstretched leg, which looked quite attractive in page boy garb. Her approach, she decided, had been too unladylike. St. Erth would prefer a more delicate female. Ermyntrude could languish as well as any other damsel, given the chance.

She was determined that she would be given the chance. "Why, the same plan we have always had! Just because Tabby keeps getting sidetracked doesn't mean the plan's at fault. One of us must parlay with Mrs. Quarles!" Now she had everyone's attention. Ermyntrude drew upon her own recent experience. "And if she won't parlay with us, then one of us must gain entry to her house and steal those letters back!"

Chapter Seventeen

Meanwhile, at the same moment that Tabby was making her confession to the Elphinstones, a very animated conversation of a different nature was underway in a pretty little villa in North Street. Involved in this rumption also were two females, both of them past their first youth. One looked awesomely respectable, in her trained walking gown of hail stone muslin, straw bonnet, and nankeen pelisse. Mrs. Quarles presented a somewhat more bizarre appearance, her voluptuous person wrapped in a fine muslin dressing gown and a mobcap of net and Brussels lace perched on her golden curls. A shawl of English cashmere was flung round her shoulders. She wore a quantity of pearls at neck and throat. Clearly, she had not been expecting to entertain callers. Nor did she appear to relish this intrusion upon her solitude.

"Lud!" the golden-haired woman said now. "You gave me a nasty turn. What do you mean, bursting in on a person like this? You might have caused me to go off in an apoplexy, or worse!"

The other woman's expression was unsympathetic. Grimly, she sat down in a black-lacquered chair. "Would you have seen me otherwise? I think not. And I also think it time we had a little heart-to-heart, Margot. About certain accounts that remain unpaid!"

Mrs. Quarles also chose to be seated, at her dressing table, with her back to her visitor. "Accounts?" she asked. "I am very sorry if some of your customers are not so prompt in paying as you might like, but I still fail to understand why you should burst in upon *me* like some avenging fury, Rose!" She glanced into her mirror, which afforded her a clear reflection not only of her own pretty face but also of her unwanted guest. "I am very sorry for it, of course—but what can I do, pray?"

Rose snorted. "You can stop playing the innocent, Margot! You know perfectly well whom those past-due accounts belong to."

Margot contemplated her own reflection now. She thought she looked very innocent, indeed. "I do?"

Rose sighed. "Cut line, do! You're under the hatches again, aren't you? Else why would you be barricaded in your bedroom like this?"

These shrewd observations caused Margot to wince. "You are an excellent creature, Rose," she said. "I have always thought so, and that is why we have rubbed along wondrous great together these several years. How sad I am to see you now grown so vulgarly inquisitive!"

"Sticks and stones!" retorted Rose. Spots of color appeared in her sallow cheeks. "You may call me as vulgar as you like, do you but pay your bills!"

Margot would have adored to pay her bills; unfortunately, she could not. This unpalatable fact she did not deem prudent to confess to one of her chief creditors. "I haven't the least notion what you are going on about!" she protested therefore. "Unless— Perhaps you have sent your accountings to the wrong address? In which case, it is hardly fair of you to hold me responsible for reckonings that have gone astray!"

Astray, was it? Rose suspected that the reckonings in question had strayed no father than her hostess's writing desk. She glanced pointedly at that item of furniture and

131

withdrew a list from her reticule. "Robe of Salisburg drugget, trimmed with gold lace; black velvet pelisse. Full evening dress with long tunic, high split collar and embroidered hem. Ball gown with sleeves of Ionic origin and palmette border at the hemline. Lilac satin spancer. Promenade dress with Tyrolean cloak and lace borders. Hooded evening cloak of purple-blue taffeta lined with rose. Indian shawl made into a dress, with its borders forming the hemline."

Margot could bear to hear no more. "Which," she interrupted, "was *not* a success!"

"And so I told you it would not be!" retorted Rose. "You haven't the figure for it. But would you listen? Not that it signifies a whit to me whether you like the gown or not. What *does* signify is that I'm wishful of being paid for it!"

Margot fidgeted with the jars and bottles on her dressing table. "Was there ever anything equal to this?" she wondered aloud. "Things have come to a very pretty pass when you feel that you must hound me, Rose. If I have failed to pay you so promptly as you might like—through some oversight! I shall remedy the situation, of course."

Rose's long nose twitched. "When?"

Unfortunately, Margot could not answer that question. "Oh, what does it matter?" she cried. "I very seriously and solemnly assure you that your accounts shall be settled in full, and soon, Rose! You act as though I were trying to cheat you. And after our long acquaintance! It is a poor way to run a business, forgetting to send out your reckonings and then dunning your customers because they have not been paid!"

Rose was too shrewd a businesswoman to be led down a blind alley. She folded her list. "You received them, right enough. Whether you opened them, I couldn't say. You'd do much better to deal upon the square with me, Margot."

Did Margot detect a note of sympathy in that flinty voice? She turned on her chair. "Very well, then, Rose! I do not scruple to tell you that everything is going as badly as possible. I vow I don't know what is to become of me! It is all the fault of this age in which we live. Perhaps Prinny may be enjoying a halcyon period with Mrs. Fitzherbert, but even he must find it difficult to ignore the scandalous behavior of his estranged wife. York consoles himself in the arms of a new ladybird for the embarrassment caused him by a mistress who trafficked in military preferments behind his back; and Sussex, who previously ran afoul of the Royal Marriage Act, is now suing his onetime wife to restrain her from calling herself duchess and using the royal arms!" She paused as if her point had been made.

If so, it had failed to reach its target. Rose failed to see what connection the goings-on of royalty had to do with her own post-obit accounts, and said so.

"Why, simply this!" responded Margot, so pleased with her clever reasoning that she abandoned her dressing table and took a turn around the room. "It is up to royalty, surely, to show us lesser mortals how we are to go on. It seems to me, Rose, that one is either miserable because one is in love or because one is not! Romance is the universal malady. Although, considering how often it goes wrong, I cannot imagine why! The state of my own affairs is such that it is very little wonder that I may have grown a teeny bit remiss about my accounts."

Rose reflected upon the tendency also of royalty to fail to pay its bills. The world, she thought, was in a shocking way. About the proclivities of royalty, she could do nothing. In her own customers, however, Rose was accustomed to instilling the fear of the Lord. Or, rather, the fear of debtors' prison. "If I was you, I'd apply to that gentleman friend who you was so wishful of pleasing when you ordered all this!'' she said, again indicating her list.

Margot glanced at that item, and guiltily away. ''I have not seen him for some time!'' She sighed. ''He does not answer my letters. I believe he is to make a most advantageous match.''

Rose was wasting her time trying to draw blood from a turnip. ''All the more reason to have a little heart-to-heart with him!'' she said. ''Gentlemen on the verge of stepping into parson's mousetrap aren't generally desirous of their brides' becoming aware of certain facts of life. Otherwise—'' She paused. Rose was not entirely without sympathy for Margot. Given a less shrewd intellect and a prettier face, she might have stood in the other woman's shoes. Business was business, however, and never in the many years they had dealt together had Margot's accounts been so far in arrears. ''I'll give you a sennight. But if you haven't made things right by then, Margot, I'll have to make application where you'd rather I would not! I'll see myself out.''

Margot paled but said nothing. She watched the seamstress exit, heard her footsteps fade away down the hall. Only when silence had again descended did Margot pick up a pretty little bibelot from off the mantelshelf and hurl it at the wall.

Her feelings somewhat relieved by the crash of china, Margot resumed her agitated pacing. She had been put at an unfair advantage, she thought resentfully; but perhaps it was better to be caught *en déshabillé* in the middle of the afternoon than to have been discovered wearing one of the costumes for which she had not paid. Not that Margot was to be censored for her failure to get dressed. In the absence of the gentlemen, the ladies may do as they wish, even to the extent of leaving off their stays. But it was not the absence of a gentleman, now, that occupied Margot's thoughts. She was entertaining grim

134

visions of an execution taking place in her house, with the carts drawn up outside her door, being piled high by her heartless creditors with all she owned in the world.

Silence settled upon the bedroom. Even the parakeet in his gilded cage ceased to sing, as if he'd caught his mistress's morose mood. The afternoon sunlight streamed through the window, playing upon the crimson and gold in the Persian-patterned carpet, warming the sphinx heads and crocodiles and serpents of the Egyptian-influenced furniture. The bedroom was filled with such curiosities. Even the dressing table and corner basin stand had not escaped lacquer work and water lilies of the Nile. Only the bed was untouched by its owner's immersion in the Egyptian craze, and it was fitted up complete with cushions in the form of a Turkish sofa, a drapery curtain in front, and girandoles on each side.

The sun glinted also off Margot's golden curls as she passed by the window—if those golden curls owned more to artifice than nature, such contrivances must surely be forgiven ladies of a certain age. She leaned over her dressing table and scrutinized her reflection, but no sign of her trouble could yet be read in her pretty, whimsical face. She wondered how long it would be before her constant worry and depression over her perennial financial crises would begin to take their toll. Not that it would matter if her flesh began to sag and wrinkle and her bright eyes dim and her hair turn gray, not if she were in debtors' prison, for who would see her there anyway?

Margot turned away from her mirror. Since she was already so depressed, it would do little harm to look for those accounts Rose was so concerned about. She fetched the brandy bottle that she customarily kept hidden in her corner basin stand and poured a liberal serving of the liquor into a glass. A pretty feather boa caught her eye, and she draped it attractively around her neck. Then she crossed the Persian-patterned carpet, sat down at the pretty little writing table of slender proportions, pushed back its tambour shutter, stared morosely at the pigeonholes overflowing with post-obit bills. She fortified herself with a sip of brandy, before repairing to her task.

And quite a task it was. Cambric petticoats and cotton chemises; day and evening gloves of white kid, Limerick, York-tan; buckram and whalebone stays; assorted hats and bonnets; reticules and tippets, and a swansdown muff. Margot was stunned to think she could owe so much, in addition to what she owed Rose Brown. Grimacing, she reached for a sheet of paper and her inkstand. With furrowed bow and lower lip caught charmingly between her teeth, she struggled to tally her accounts.

The afternoon hours had lengthened when Margot gave up her reckoning. Though she'd reached no grand total, she knew her finances were seriously deranged. There was nothing new in this; she'd been living far beyond her income for months. Before, however, she had found some way out of her financial difficulties. "Oh, bother!" she said aloud in bitter tones, causing the parakeet dozing in its gilded cage to start and very nearly tumble off his perch. "I haven't a feather to fly with, Dickie!" Dickie ruffled his own feathers irritably, and she reached for a stack of missives that had arrived by the latest post. Margot sighed, expecting more of the same. She was not disappointed.

Then she glimpsed a familiar handwriting; the same handwriting contained on a ribbon-bound packet of letters that were ripe with such effusions as "difficult to believe in my good fortune" and "never more pleased with anything in all my life." Margot smiled wistfully over these pretty sentiments. Her gaze lingered especially upon "You are not mortal, but divine."

So he had not forgotten her entirely, not altogether closed his heart. It seemed her troubles were at an end.

Happily, Margot opened the latter. " 'Notice to quit,' " she read aloud. With considerable effort, Margot quelled an impulse to throw further objects at the wall. Instead, she drained her brandy glass, pushed back her chair. She walked to the window, drew the curtain aside and gazed down into the noisy street. Nowhere could compare with Brighton in its display of vehicles. Often she had derived considerable entertainment from watching the procession of coaches and phaetons, curricles and buggies and gigs; had, in the pleasure of observing such notables as Lord Petersham and Mr. Tommy Onslaw and Sir John Lade, not minded so very much that she had no carriage of her own. Now even this small pleasure was to be taken from her. She was to be forced to quit this little villa that she had come to think of as her own. How very unpleasant it was to be the plaything of fortune. She sniffled, then sneezed. Dickie, nearly deafened by this outburst, voiced an indignant squawk.

"Oh, hush, you wretched bird!" Margot was indeed desperate, to seek sympathy from a creature that had had scant interest in anything beyond the boundaries of its own cage. And she was also overwrought, so that in the absence of another human being she would talk to a bird. "I am expected meekly to pack my belongings and creep away," she muttered as she walked back to her desk. "Under cover no doubt of darkness, so that no one may see!" Under other circumstances, she might have done so. Margot remembered that the owner of this pretty villa had not been unkind to her in the past.

She also remembered Rose's threats. Needs must when the devil drove. Geoffrey would not easily forget her at any rate. Once more she reached out for her inkstand.

Margot's back was to the door. When she heard it open, she thought her tormentor had returned. "Not another word!" said Margot. "You *did* promise me a sennight to bring my accounts current, Rose!"

137

There came a throat clearing, and a panting noise, and a scuffling sound. Margot could not imagine Rose being their source. She turned in her chair. Not Rose stood in the doorway, but a young woman dressed in black, who appeared to be grappling with a large and most unattractive hound.

"Oh, do sit down!" cried the young woman in exasperated tones. The dog merely wagged his tail more energetically. "I already am sitting," remarked Margot, amused. "Do you think you might tell me who you are?"

Tabby flushed with embarrassment. She attempted to render Lambchop less a nuisance by forcing his haunches down on the floor and then keeping them in that position by playing her foot upon his tail. She felt very hot and tired and cross. Ermyntrude and Drusilla had wished to accompany Tabby on this excursion, and she had put them off by agreeing to bring Lambchop with her as protection against a possible meeting with a certain rakehell. As a consequence, Tabby had made the acquaintance of many alleys and byways that she'd had no wish to explore, and was short of breath.

"I'm sorry to burst in on you like this!" Tabby said now to the lady whose acquaintance she had so long sought to make. "Your servant told me to come along upstairs!"

Margot reflected that her servants had been a great deal nicer in their behavior in the days when they were being paid. This young woman could hardly be a bailiff, however. She was also not experienced with dogs, judging by the manner in which the beast was currently wrapping her up in his leash.

Margot rose and crossed the room to inspect the situation at closer hand. "Oh, dear!" said Tabby, as she realized how the woman was dressed. "You aren't receiving company."

"Apparently I am," said Margot dryly. She turned her attention to Lambchop. "Sit!"

So startled was Lambchop by this stern command that he instantly obeyed. Tabby almost did likewise. She stared at Mrs. Quarles's face, whimsical beneath her ridiculously flattering mobcap. "Oh, my God!" gasped Tabby. "Mama!"

Chapter Eighteen

Mr. Peregrine Smithton strolled through the streets of Brighton. He wore a very disdainful air. Indeed, in his high heels and even higher cravat, his coat and breeches of a daring spotted material, Perry resembled a very superior giraffe. He had not changed his opinion of Brighton. Not for Perry were such amenities as the city offered. He would allow himself to be nibbled to death by ducks before he hired a bathing machine. Only the fact that he was known to detest Brighton accounted for his presence now. His unhappy creditors would not think to look for him there.

At that very moment, as if in defiance of his reflections, someone called Perry's name. He looked somewhat frantically about, in search of a hiding place. Nothing suitable presented itself. "Perry!" came the voice again, closer now. Perry sighed, raised his quizzing glass, and turned to meet his fate. But it was only Vivien Sanders, beckoning from the high seat of his cabriolet. Perry let out a great sigh of relief and went to greet his friend.

"Dash it!" he said as he climbed up into the cabriolet. "You needn't scare a fellow half out of his wits! Which reminds me, I've a bone to pick with you, Viv! Though dashed if I can think what it is!"

"And I with you!" Mr. Sanders refrained from commenting on his friend's costume. "Tell me what you know about Mrs. Quarles!"

"Quarles?" Perry turned his head, with difficulty, to stare at his friend. "Who the deuce is that?"

Vivien looked sardonic. "A very unusual high-flyer, whom apparently you knew well enough to give your room at the inn!"

Perry was very confused. Erratic though his memory might be, he was almost positive that he numbered no high-flyers among his acquaintance. After all, he wasn't in the petticoat line, and gentlemen who weren't in the petticoat line didn't usually rub shoulders with females of that sort.

When his friend continued to be silent, Vivien mentioned a certain inn in a bucolic setting and a boxing match that had been held nearby. *"Now,"* he inquired impatiently, "do you recall?"

Indeed Perry did. "Rosters!" he said triumphantly. "Prizefights! And I think it very poor of you to drag me out into the country, which you know I detest of all things, and then fail to meet me!"

Vivien supposed it would be even more poor-spirited of him to throttle his uncooperative friend. "I did show up," he said, "but the hour was late, and you had already gone. And then I found Mrs. Quarles in your room."

Perry blushed at the implications of this statement. "You did not!" he protested. "You couldn't have! Stands to reason: I don't have any traffic with ladybirds!"

Vivien was made even more cross by Perry's stubbornness. "Must everyone try to pull the wool over my eyes?" he snapped. "You know her, all right, because she said you did, and *I* know she's no better than she should be!"

Perry had recalled by now to whom he'd lent his room.

"I didn't know Quarles was her name. I thought it was something else altogether, because of old Tolly, you know!" he said, in self-defense. "And I certainly didn't know she was a lightskirt. Are you certain of it, Viv? She told me she wasn't any such thing."

Who was "old Tolly"? Vivien decided he'd rather not know. "She is most definitely a high-flyer. She even informed me that she advertised."

Perry goggled. Then he recalled that Tabby had said something of the sort. But he thought she had advertised for a post. Although he supposed that a ladybird was as necessary an adjunct to some gentlemen as a governess. Who would have thought Tabby so enterprising? "Zounds!" he said.

Vivien urged his horse to a quicker pace. "To tell the truth, I had trouble believing it myself," he confessed. "She looks like a respectable female. And acts like one, as well. Except for her fondness for blackmail!"

"Blackmail?" echoed Perry. This was going too far. While his imagination might stretch to accept old Tolly's niece in the guise of a soiled dove, it balked at blackmail. Perhaps some error had been made. "Tell you, what, Viv: Describe the chit!"

"Brown hair," Vivien said promptly. "Big eyes. A pretty face and figure. A delightful sense of the absurd. An original, not at all in the ordinary way. Provoking, provocative. Thoroughly adorable," he concluded, with a sigh.

"That's her," Perry conceded. "Except for the adorable part, and I wouldn't know about that. Not that I mean to say she ain't! Thought she was a pretty-behaved female myself. A good sort of girl!"

"That good sort of girl," retorted Vivien, "is my sister's fiancé's *petite amie*."

"Your sister's fiancé's—" Perry stared suspiciously at his friend. "Are you trying to flummery me?"

"I wish I were!" said Vivien. "My sister's fiancé apparently goes about seducing females right and left. As for Mrs. Quarels, you were not the only one to be mistaken in her, Perry. I, too, seem to have lost the ability to distinguish between a soiled dove and one who is not!"

"*Mrs.* Quarles!" Perry cried in triumph. "That explains it! I've been cudgeling my brain about that queer business of her name. She must have acquired a husband somewhere! I wonder where he is." Perry recalled that, when he encountered her at the inn, Tabby had been dressed in black. He thought she said that it was old Tolly who'd popped off, but perhaps he'd been confused. Well, there was no point in further puzzling his head over it. "Viv, what are you going to do?"

"Call him out!" Vivien said promptly. "Cut out his gizzard and use it for daylight! Hell and the devil confound it, Perry, I don't know. Gus cannot be permitted to marry Elphinstone, of course. What a proper take-in! I would have said there wasn't an ounce of vice in the chit."

Vivien was in the devil of a pucker. Erratic as Perry's memory might be, he was prepared to take his oath that he had never seen his friend in such a state before. That he did so now was a source of wonderment. Could Vivien be foxed? A glass of Madeira would have elevated Perry's own spirits considerably, but the amenities of the cabriolet did not extend to intoxicants. "Tell you what, Viv!" Perry observed. "Seems to me you're in a bad way!"

"I am *not* in a bad way!" Vivien retorted irritably. "I don't know why you should say such a thing. I am merely very angry at the way that I—that is, my sister—has been taken in."

Perry contemplated his spotted jacket sleeve. He might not have been needle-witted, but he knew chalk from cheese. "What about the divine Sara?" he asked.

143

Vivien hadn't thought about the divine Sara for some days and did not care to be reminded now of his neglect. "What about Sara?" he retorted irritably. "Devil take it, Perry, I offered to take her into my keeping, and she boxed my ears!"

"Boxed your ears?" Half strangled by his high cravat, Perry turned sideways on the carriage seat. "You astonish me, Viv! I'd have thought that such an offer would've suited her to a cow's thumb. But it queers me as to which female you're on the dangle for!"

Vivien had no doubts in that direction. "Not Sara!" he said. "Mrs. Quarles. That is, it was she who boxed my ears. I'm not on the dangle for anyone—no, nor intend to be again, once this business is finished!"

Perry did not again accuse his friend of telling whiskers, though this was obviously the case. He could guess what had taken place. Vivien was accustomed to being very much admired by the weaker sex. But instead of administering to his vanity, Tabby had instead cut up all his hopes. Perry was astonished that such an unexceptionable miss could send Vivien Sanders tumbling head over heels, when so many great beauties had tried to do precisely that and failed. Clearly, Perry had underestimated her. Or perhaps it was simply that he did not understand the game of hearts.

Vivien was made uncomfortable by his friend's silence. "I have *not* taken a marked fancy to her!" he said, in case Perry had failed to understand. "I'm hardly such a flat. I don't care a button for Mrs. Quarles. It's my sister I'm concerned about."

Of course Vivien was concerned about his sister. Perry didn't doubt that for a moment. Nor did he doubt that his friend was fast in the grip of petticoat fever. Perry was very sorry to see Vivien made so unhappy. He could not help but feel responsible. Had Perry not played the Good

Samaritan, Vivien would never have met the deceitful Mrs. Quarles.

Vivien interrupted these thoughts. "Devil take it, Perry, has the cat got your tongue?"

Was there a feline in the cabriolet? Perry turned his head for a quick and painful look about. Then he realized that Vivien had merely used a figure of speech. "I was just thinking! About your sister!" Perry retorted with wounded dignity. "Viv, what're you going to do? Call out Elphinstone?"

"Gus wouldn't like the scandal," Vivien retorted grimly. "And so I must try another tack. That is, *we* will! I finally learned where Mrs. Quarles resides—in a house owned by Elphinstone. Apparently he's had her in his keeping all this time."

There seemed to be no end to Tabby's scheming. She'd duped him, too, Perry realized. He wouldn't have given her his room otherwise. Belatedly, he realized the full impact of Vivien's words. "We?" he gasped. *"Now?"*

"Yes, we!" retorted Vivien. "Now! A matter of such importance can hardly be left dangling. My poor sister's health is not good at the best of times."

Perry thought his own health would suffer were he made to witness a confrontation so unpleasant as what must take place. "I want no part of it!" he retorted. "That is, it ain't for me to shove my oar into your personal business. Or your sister's! She wouldn't like it, Viv. Stands to reason she wouldn't, because she don't like me above half!"

"No, she doesn't," agreed Vivien, "and here's your chance to change her mind. Do you but persuade Mrs. Quarles not to make a scandal, Gus will be your friend for life." He scowled. *"Not* that I intend to see her resume her romance with Elphinstone!"

Perry was not persuaded. "Wish I could help you out!" he said. "I'd like it above all things. But I just

145

remembered, I have an urgent appointment! I'm already late!''

Vivien's scowl deepened. "Can *you* be in on this business, Perry? I would not have thought you could be persuaded to help a doxy fleece one of your friends.''

"Well, I like that!'' Perry retorted indignantly. "Next you'll accuse *me* of being a cursed rum touch! For your information, Viv, my pockets ain't that far to let! And even if they was, I wouldn't! *I*'m not the one who allows ladybirds to persuade me to do things I shouldn't, adorable or not!''

Vivien ignored this latter insinuation. "Good. Then you'll accompany me,'' he said.

There was no escape, unless Perry hurled himself out of the swiftly moving cabriolet, which would have caused considerable damage to both his person and his suit. Resigned, he settled back in his seat. "Where do you know Mrs. Quarles from?'' asked Vivien; then added, before Perry could respond, "Never mind! We're here.''

Perry climbed down from the cabriolet, watched Vivien pay a street urchin to walk his horse. Once more, he tried for freedom. "Here for the waters!'' he said earnestly. "Need to rusticate! M'sawbones said I couldn't stand any excitement! Peace and quiet, you know! Tell you what, Viv, I'll just wait for you here, by the door.''

"The devil you will!'' Vivien took firm grip on Perry's sleeve and knocked at the door. "You are going to speak with Mrs. Quarles. You know the wench; perhaps she will listen to you. Don't you wish to earn Gus's undying gratitude and mine?''

Perry had no great desire to earn anyone's gratitude. He wished only for a life unencumbered by individuals stricken down by petticoat fever and tradesmen desirous of receiving immediate payment. But it was not to be. Perry could not abandon his friend, and certainly not while Vivien had such a firm grasp on his expensive, as-yet-unpaid-for sleeve. "People don't usually listen when I talk," he said doubtfully. "Maybe no one's at home. Don't despair, Viv! We'll come back another day!"

Even as he spoke, the door opened. A maidservant looked the callers over, head to toe. Perry's elegant attire caused her to blink, but then Vivien caught her eye. She stepped back and let them enter. "Madam is in the bedroom," she said. "First room to your left at the top of the stairs." Grimly, Vivien set out toward the doorway. Forlornly, Perry followed in his wake.

Chapter Nineteen

Margot contemplated her visitor. "You needn't," she said sternly, "try to run a rig with me, my girl! I've run a fair number of rigs myself in my day, so there's no use you wasting your time trying to teach your grandmother to suck eggs."

Tabby's knees felt weak. She sat down, uninvited, on a black-lacquered chair. "Not grandmother, Mama! How the devil—er, how do you come to be *here*? Uncle Tolly had the impression you'd gone to the Continent."

"I did go to Continent," retorted Margot, startled into telling the truth. "Unfortunately my, er, traveling companion abandoned me there."

Tabby had scant sympathy to spare for her errant parent. "It is no more than you deserve! For treating Papa in that shabby way."

The chit dared to scold her? "Your papa would have driven a bishop to the bottle!" Margot replied. And then the full import of this odd conversation burst upon her. This impertinent miss must indeed be her abandoned child. As if existence were not already sufficiently complicated! Margot did not feel prepared to deal with yet another complication. Gracefully, she swooned across the bed.

Tabby suspected that swoon was no more genuine than

the color of her mama's curls, was instead a ruse to prevent further conversation taking place. Tabby, however, had a great deal yet to say. She glanced around the room. Her glance fell on the feather boa. With a certain grim satisfaction, Tabby removed it from her mama's neck and approached the fireplace.

As Tabby bent to her task, the door was flung open, and two gentlemen entered the room. Lambchop, freed by Margot's swoon from her command to remain seated, sped to greet the visitors enthusiastically. The gentlemen swore. Tabby bit her lip, caught off guard. Vivien's sudden appearance in this setting left her both angry and confused. As for his companion— "Perry!" she gasped.

Perry lowered his quizzing glass, through which he had been inspecting a certain large and, he suspected, misbegotten hound. He was very uncomfortable at finding himself in a lady's boudoir. But he had agreed to speak with Mrs. Quarles on Vivien's behalf, and the sooner he put the ordeal behind him, the quicker he could go away.

"You *don't* look like a ladybird!" he said therefore to Tabby in very severe tones. "Yes, and I distinctly recall you told me you was nothing of the sort. It's not the thing to go about telling clankers, my girl! It gives people a very poor sort of opinion, you know! Although I daresay it's even *less* the thing to put oneself in a gentleman's keeping. Dashed if I can think what old Tolly would say!" He paused to contemplate this matter. Tabby made a strangling sound. Perry thought she looked very pathetic, crouched there on the floor.

"Daresay it ain't your fault!" he said generously. "Doubtless it's all to be laid at the door of this Quarles fellow, who sounds like a cursed bad fish! But blackmail— who'd have thought it? I tell you, it just won't do!" He somewhat spoiled his lecture, then, by wrinkling his nose. "What the deuce is that smell?"

Tabby snatched her mama's boa away from the fire that

she had lit, burned feathers being considered an excellent restorative for a swoon. If ever Tabby had felt like swooning, it was now, with Vivien standing in the doorway and scowling at her like a thundercloud. But, of course, she could allow herself no such luxury. Instead, she stood up awkwardly, the burned boa in her hand.

Unlike Perry, Vivien felt no pity. He had been very worried when his rage abated and he realized he'd left this young woman to walk unescorted all the way back to town. Now he was perversely very angry to see her safe. "Yes," he said impatiently. "What have you to say for yourself—Mrs. Quarles?"

Mrs. Quarles had a great many things to say and a great curiosity about this invasion of her bedroom. Additionally, it pained her that her daughter should be so extravagant as to burn a boa for which Margot had not yet paid. "I said sit, you wretched beast!" she uttered, in tones so disapproving that poor Lambchop immediately slunk beneath the bed. Gracefully, Margot rose. "Can a lady have no privacy even in her own bedchamber?" she inquired.

"*Your* bedchamber?" Vivien swung round to stare at this second female. His experienced gaze moved over golden curls and muslin dressing gown, cashmere shawl and pearls. An appreciative gleam lit his eyes. "Oho!" he said.

Tabby understood that tone. She contemplated the burned feathers. A restorative would definitely be in order if she was forced to watch Mr. Sanders flirt with her mama. Perry, on the other hand, understood nothing, except that he was in the presence of a female in a state of undress. "Dashed if I know what's happening here!" he muttered. "Who is this Quarles fellow, anyway?"

Margot was much more interested in this handsome green-eyed devil, who was obviously in a temper, and what had brought him into her boudoir. But she was not one to treat any gentleman caller ill. "Quarles was a mis-

150

take," she admitted. "His mind was of a mean and little structure, and his pockets were to let, both of which unfortunate circumstances I discovered too late! He died of an apoplexy not long after, upon seeing the size of my mantua maker's bill. I fear my heart ruled my head." She glanced at Perry. "You will understand."

Perry took this comment personally and blushed brighter still. "No! That is, I ain't in the petticoat line!"

Margot looked interested. "How very curious! You must explain to me why not, someday. But first, do you gentlemen think you might explain to me who you are?" Her curious glance returned to Vivien. "And why you have invaded my boudoir? Not that you aren't perfectly welcome! I am never more comfortable than when there is a gentleman in the house."

Vivien spared Perry an answer. "Perhaps it will simplify matters if I explain that I am Lady Grey's brother, Mrs. Quarles."

"Ah." Margot supposed it had been too much to hope that so very attractive a gentleman would not have impediments of some sort. With a charmingly rueful expression, she sat down at her writing desk. "So this is in the way of being a business call."

Vivien sat down also, on the black-lacquered chair. "Regrettably, yes."

How could Tabby be jealous of her mama? Still, she took consolation from the fact that Vivien's smile did not reach his eyes. He glanced at her then, and Tabby looked quickly away. "The business of blackmail," he added. "Apparently I have been asking the wrong person for your price."

Margot glanced also at her daughter, who was clutching the feather boa as if it were a lifeline of some sort. So Tabitha was acquainted with this devilishly attractive rogue? He certainly was astute. She had not yet posted her letter. "Ah, yes. One must be practical." Margot prepared to negotiate.

Perhaps some members of the group had achieved enlightenment from this latter exchange, but Perry was still feeling very much in the dark. Nor was he certain he craved enlightenment. He followed Tabby across the room to stand by the parakeet's gilded cage. She seemed to have an affinity for feathered creatures, he thought, watching her clutch the singed boa. "What did you do with the rooster?" he asked, by way of making polite conversation. She looked blank. "You know, the one that was following at your heels like a tantony pig!"

Tabby was in no mood for polite conversation. Her attention was fixed on her mama and Mr. Sanders, embarked on an animated exchange. "I wish I'd never met you or that rooster!" she said rudely. "No, nor your friend."

Sat the wind in that quarter? Perry was stunned to discover that, despite the benefits of a classical education, Tabby was no more prudent than less learned members of her sex. He could not help but pity her folly. Clearly, she and Vivien would not suit. For one thing, Vivien would never forgive a female who'd boxed his ears. "You should have said your name isn't Minchin!" he said. "It's caused the devil of a lot of a confusion, your not telling me your name was Quarles."

Tabby didn't correct Perry's error. She wasn't at all certain about the business of her name. If her mama's name was Quarles, then did not that name also apply to Tabby in some wise?

The same point had occurred to Vivien. "If *you* are Mrs. Quarles," he said now to Margot, "then who the devil is *she* that she goes about using your name and negotiating in your place?"

Margot, too, was curious. "Who, indeed?"

"I did not!" interrupted Tabby defensively. "It was Vi

152

vien—er, Mr. Sanders who insisted on trying to buy me off. All I ever wished to do was speak out on Sir Geoffrey's behalf, because I believe he has been treated very shabbily.'' She gazed defiantly at her mama. ''Both by Lady Grey and by you, Ma—''

''Margot!'' supplied that lady smoothly. She was not in the habit of admitting that she was old enough to have adult offspring. ''So you must also call me, gentlemen; I'm sure we shall become great friends.''

''Certainly we shall!'' said Vivien. ''Do you but let Elphinstone off your hook.''

Perry roused from contemplation of the parakeet. ''I don't understand!'' he said to Tabby. ''If you ain't Elphinstone's fancy piece—which you obviously ain't, because *she* is!—then why should you care a button whether or not he's in the suds?''

''Yes.'' Vivien, too, turned to look at Tabby. ''Why should you?''

It was the perfect moment for explanations. Tabby found herself tongue-tied. Vivien's brooding glance moved from her to Margot. There was a faint resemblance between the two women. The resemblance would be even greater, he realized, if the younger of the ladies were to age a good ten years and dye her hair gold. How foolishly disappointed he was to realize she was what he'd thought her, after all. And she had dared accuse *him* of double-dealing! If she was no high-flyer herself, then she was related to one and additionally involved in the very nasty business of blackmail.

It was that business, of course, which was his main concern here. ''So you are kin. You have done yourself no good with your charade.'' His chill gaze moved to Margot. ''The pair of you do not appear to agree on the subject of Sir Geoffrey Elphinstone. Your sister has assured me repeatedly of his kindness, whereas you, ma'am, seem to hold him in very low regard.''

"Fiddlestick!" retorted Margot, curious about Tabby's association with Sir Geoffrey and pleased that the discriminating Mr. Sanders should think she and Tabby of an age. "I hold none of my, er, friends in low regard, even after friendship runs its course; and I'm sure I'd remain as fond of Sir Geoffrey as anyone had he not acted so callously." She looked misty-eyed. "We were wondrous great together once. He would have done anything for me."

Tabby could no longer remain silent. "And this is how you repay him? By throwing a spanner into his romance?"

Margot was very hurt by these accusations. She picked up Sir Geoffrey's love letters and clasped them to her breast. "I'm sure I meant to do no such thing. I wish Geoffrey every happiness. You do not believe me. You think me cruel and callous, I can see it in your eyes, but the truth is that I had a great regard for Geoffrey before he gave me a disgust by putting me on notice to—well! That's neither here nor there. But there is no use arguing with me on this head because I shall not change my mind!"

"I see." Vivien stood. "so you are determined to publish, then."

"Publish?" Margot glanced at the ribbon-bound packet. A look of immense satisfaction settled on her pretty face. "What a splendid notion! Perhaps the threat of recrimination may persuade Geoffrey to adopt a more reasonable stand. He will pay me *not* to publish, and thus I may fulfill my ambition to be beforehand with the world. How fortunate it is that you came to call on me! I am not of a managing nature, so I would never have thought to take so direct an approach."

Vivien looked as though he wished to gnash his teeth. "I am sorry to hear you say so," he snapped, "Because of course I cannot permit you to do such a thing. I fear our next meeting will be under even less pleasant circumstances, ladies. Perhaps, if you may not be dissuaded from

154

your purpose, in a court of law. Perry? Do you go with me?''

With alacrity, the unhappy Mr. Smithton detached himself from the parakeet's cage. In his opinion, something about this business was very queer. Indeed, he wouldn't have been surprised to learn Vivien had taken a nest of bees in his head.

He followed his friend out of the room. "Well, Viv, that's that! It went off fairly well, don't you think? That is, you have everything under control. Which is a very good thing, because I've just recalled that I have urgent business elsewhere—m'aunt, the one who's forever threatening to cut me out of her will! You know what my memory is! Won't hold no more water than a sieve! So I'd best off and do the pretty, don't you know?'' His voice faded as the gentlemen moved down the hall.

Tabby moved to stand at the window of her mama's boudoir. "What a pickle!" she said bitterly. "Have you no conscience, Mama?''

Margot winced. "Must you call me that? I understand that you might be a teeny bit angry with me for running off all those years ago, but I had good reason. Or so it seemed at the time. Your father was impossible to live with. He was jealous and neglectful, and peevish to boot, which is a dreadful combination for a woman of my temperament to be married to. The truth is that we didn't suit—which is obvious, is it not, because if we *had* suited, I would hardly have run away! And it is just as well I did, because at least I was spared seeing myself widowed because he *would* ride that accursed horse!'' Her tone softened. "I read of your uncle's illness. You have my sympathy. He was all that his brother was not.''

Tabby's main concern now was not her parents' ill-fated marriage. "Sir Geoffrey offered me a place when my uncle died,'' she said. "As governess to his daughters. I am in his debt.''

155

"And you say *I* am in a pickle!" Margot moved to join Tabby at the window. "Not that Vivien Sanders isn't a deucedly handsome sort. Cursedly ill-tempered, too, a quality which I personally admire in a gentleman!"

Tabby didn't wish to hear her mama sing Vivien's praises. "I ask you, as your daughter, that you leave Sir Geoffrey in peace."

Margot gestured toward the post-obit bills strewn across her desk. "I would like to oblige you, child. Truly. Unfortunately, I cannot ignore these."

"I see." How disappointing it was to discover that her mama was selfish and conscienceless. "I am here as Sir Geoffrey's emissary. He wishes you to tell me what you want from him."

But Margot was not entirely without conscience. "Lud!" she said. "As if I would involve you in such business, child! You may tell Geoffrey that he must speak with me himself."

"Then we have nothing more to say to one another," responded Tabby, and turned toward the door. Politely, Margot requested that she leave behind the feather boa. Tabby laid the boa carefully on her mama's dressing table. Margot had turned to gaze out the window. Tabby tucked the ribbon-bound packet of letters into her reticule, then speedily exited her mama's house.

Chapter Twenty

Lady Grey was in her drawing room, which had taken on the atmosphere of an invalid's chamber. No smell of burned feathers fouled the air, but on the table at Gus's elbow were numerous bottles containing every restorative remedy known to man. Servants tiptoed in and out with a procession of delicacies intended to tempt the invalid's appetite: barley water, chicken panada, broth of eel. At this particular moment, she was sipping a chocolate cup of Dr. Ratcliff's restorative pork jelly, seasoned with nutmeg and salt and mace. In her lap was a newspaper, in which she had been reading an account of a phantasmagoria that had recently taken place at the Pavilion, complete with a Storm of Thunder and Lightning and Rain, and a Ghastly Phantom of Death. Lady Grey had done a great deal of reading these past few days, seeking to divert herself with such light fare of *The Lady's Magazine,* intended for the use and amusement of the fair sex; and, alternately, the works of Chateaubriand.

Alas, none of these diversions had been successful in preventing Lady Grey from, as her abigail succinctly put it, fretting her guts to fiddle strings. She knew she had grown quite haggard. Not that it mattered; there was no one to see her, nor would there be anyone again. Gus was done with romance. Did she recover from her heartbreak, she would devote herself to good works.

Footsteps sounded in the hallway. Augusta looked eagerly at the door. Truth be told, she was growing tired of her own company, and would welcome an opportunity to set aside the various literary works with which she had halfheartedly been improving her mind.

Mr. Sanders walked into the room. So very grim was his expression that his sister realized immediately that something was seriously amiss. "Vivien! Whatever is the matter?" she cried.

He did not answer her directly, but flung himself into a chair. "I should have known what she was from the beginning!" he muttered. "No respectable female would have stayed unchaperoned in an inn filled to the rafters with sporting gentlemen!"

August wondered if her brother might not benefit from some restorative pork jelly. She did not make the offer, knowing all too well what he thought of her quackery. "You are in need of some refreshment, Vivien!" She rang for a servant and, when her summons was answered, gestured toward her cup. "Another, please!" Then she turned back to her brother. "What inn? What female? Although I am certain you are correct in your assessment of the situation, Vivien, it sounds very queer to me!"

"I wish I might be so certain." Vivien ran his fingers through his hair. "The devil in it is that she *does* look and act like a respectable female. But she cannot be, or she would not be mixed up in this odious business. I vow I don't know what to think!"

Nor did Augusta, who had never before seen her brother take a distempered freak. "Who?" she asked again. "Not Mrs. Quarles?"

Vivien laughed harshly. "Correct! *Not* Mrs. Quarles! The truth is, Gus, that I was properly hoodwinked by a pernicious little tart."

158

"A—er!" In her perturbation upon hearing such language, Lady Grey picked up her newspaper and used it as a fan.

Vivien was oblivious of his sister's discomfort. "I suppose it was no more than I deserved that a straw damsel should trick me into thinking she fancied me."

Lady Grey fanned herself harder. "Should you be telling me this, Vivien? It does not seem proper that you should speak with your sister about your liaisons with females of that sort!"

"The devil with your propriety!" retorted Vivien. "There was no liaison, anyway. It was all a hum, and I was properly taken in." He frowned. "Though I still am not certain as to what end!"

August was uncertain also, and additionally perplexed. "I didn't know you were acquainted with Mrs. Quarles."

Again that sarcastic laugh. "I'm not! But I've known a hundred of her sort. Selfish, heartless hussies who care for nothing but to feather their own nests."

August thought back to her own meeting with Mrs. Quarles. Something about her brother's remarks did not ring true. "I hold no brief for the creature," she said, "but she seemed a great deal more concerned with Geoffrey than with herself."

Vivien had not considered this. Now that he did so, he could only conclude that Elphinstone had been involved not only with Mrs. Quarles but her sister as well. "Degenerate! Positively *depraved*!" he said.

"You refine too much upon it, surely!" Augusta was growing increasingly confused. "I do not mean to defend Mrs. Quarles, but it is Geoffrey who is at fault, surely; she is scarce more than a child. When I spoke with her—"

"You didn't speak with her!" interrupted Vivien. "You—"

"Well, really, Vivien!" interrupted Augusta, in her own turn. "Even though I may be prey to nervous upsets

I am *not* subject to disorders of the mind. I know perfectly well that I *did* speak to her and in this very room, and for you to infer otherwise is exceedingly unkind!"

Vivien was currently on the verge of a nervous disorder of his own. "Lay all those bristles!" he advised. "I wasn't inferring anything, except that the female you spoke with wasn't Mrs. Quarles!"

"Wasn't!" Augusta blinked. "But she said—"

"Whatever she said, you may be sure it wasn't true!" Vivien drummed his fingers on the arm of his chair. "Before this accursed business, I thought myself a knowing one. Now I wonder if I'm not a flat! I suspect I've been royally diddled—perhaps we both have! And I'd pay a pretty penny to find out why. I'll stake my oath the wench had no intention to publish until I put it into her head."

"Publish?" Lady Grey echoed weakly, reaching for her vinaigrette. "*You*—"

"Not on purpose!" Vivien protested. "I thought that was what she intended all along. The devil, Gus! Don't go off into your high fidgets now. We were only trying to help you, after all."

Lady Grey looked warily at her brother. "*We?*"

"Perry went with me. He knows the wench." No longer able to remain seated, Vivien rose to pace the floor.

"Perry knows Mrs. Quarles?" Augusta was astonished. She had thought Mr. Smithton too much the dandy to view females in the ordinary way.

"Not Mrs. Quarles, but the other one," said Vivien. "The female you met. It seems the pair of them are at loggerheads. Mrs. Quarles wishes to bleed Elphinstone dry, and the other wishes she will not."

Augusta dropped her vinaigrette. "Then Geoffrey didn't ruin that poor child!"

Vivien gazed into the fireplace. "As to that, I couldn't say. At any rate, she's not Mrs. Quarles."

Color bloomed in Augusta's cheeks. "This Mrs.

160

Quarles, she is older, then? Than the female who was here?''

Vivien, intent on his own unhappy thoughts, was unaware of the intensity of his sister's interest. "At least ten years, perhaps fifteen or more.''

"Ha!'' cried Lady Grey, with such exultation that Vivien turned to stare. "Then Geoffrey *isn't* one of the wicked, after all!''

Lady Grey's mind was clearly overheated. Vivien surveyed the various medications on the table by her side. Since he could not guess which would prove most effective, he offered common sense instead. "What the devil is this nonsense, Gus? Just because you met the wrong female doesn't mean the situation has changed. It's a very nasty business and promises to get even nastier. Your betrothal to Elphinstone was common knowledge, which means that your name must also be bruited about on every tongue.''

Augusta was not paying strict attention. "Oh, fudge!'' she said. "Perry may be a slow-top and a fribble, but surely he may be trusted not to tell tales!''

"I am not referring to Perry.'' Vivien spoke very slowly so that his sister might understand. "I am referring to Mrs. Quarles's determination to publish Elphinstone's love letters. That must make a dreadful scandal, Gus.''

Love letters? Sir Geoffrey had written no such stuff to her. Lady Grey felt very sad. Perhaps she would sink into a fatal decline and thus spare herself the embarrassment that such publication must cause.

The servant returned then with a second chocolate cup, which Augusta presented to Vivien. Though Vivien had stronger refreshment in mind, he did not wish to be rude. He took a sip of the beverage and grimaced. "What the devil is *this*?'' he inquired.

Lady Grey gazed blankly at the cup. Her memory had been adversely affected by the several shocks she had so

161

recently received. Then she recalled her concern over her brother's health. "It is very good for you!" she said sternly. "I find it most beneficial! But if you do not want it, Vivien, pass it over here!"

Without comment, Vivien did so. Augusta sipped from the cup. She recalled what her visitor—and if not Mrs. Quarles, who *was* the girl?—had said about Sir Geoffrey's health. "Poor Geoffrey!" she said aloud "His nerves will never stand the disgrace."

Poor Geoffrey? Vivien thought his sister's afflictions, imagined and otherwise, must finally have turned her grain. "You waste your pity!" he said curtly. "Elphinstone brought this down upon himself. Damned if I know what possessed you, Gus, to take up with a cursed profligate!"

This was too harsh, surely? Lady Grey eyed her brother over the top of her chocolate cup. "I can perfectly understand why *I* am out of charity with Geoffrey, but I do *not* understand why you have taken him in such dislike. Gracious, Vivien, you have not even met the man!"

Vivien could not explain to his sister what he did not fully understand himself. "How can you defend him?" he countered. "It is no more than Elphinstone deserves that his doxy should demand that he meet her price."

"No more than he deserves?" Even from a beloved brother, this was too much to be borne! "This from *you*, Vivien? Why, I daresay you have had a great many more doxies in your keeping than poor Geoffrey has! Indeed, if he were more experienced, this probably would not have come about!"

This from his so-proper sister? Vivien scowled. "What's got into you, Gus? You had nothing good to say for Elphinstone, just days past."

"Yes," said Augusta, quite reasonably, "but as it turns out, he didn't seduce that child! I have been thinking and thinking, and it seems to me now that you were correct

162

and I *was* a great deal too quick to judge. Gentlemen must have their little, er, indiscretions; it is the way of the world! I believe I am sufficiently large-minded to forgive a minor peccadillo! Yes, and so I must tell Geoffrey!'' She flung aside her shawl.

Vivien, alas, had also suffered a change of heart. ''You'll do no such thing! Have you failed to understand the situation? Even if Elphinstone buys the creature off, there is bound to be a scandal, Gus!''

Lady Grey took another sip of her restorative pork jelly. ''Why?''

Vivien stared at her. ''Why what?''

''Why will there be a scandal? If Geoffrey buys her off? The purpose of which surely would be to prevent a scandal taking place?'' Augusta was used to thinking her brother needle-witted. Apparently she had been wrong.

Vivien thought his sister was being deliberately obtuse. It was very bad of her to provoke him at this time. ''Mrs. Quarles is bent on mischief. Take my word on it,'' he replied. ''But I've informed her she shan't be permitted to get away with it, even if it requires taking the whole business into a court of law.''

''A court of law!'' Lady Grey thrust aside her chocolate cup with such force that pork jelly splattered onto the sofa and the floor. ''Have you taken leave of your senses, Vivien? Wouldn't *that* give the gossip mongers a field day! Moreover, what business is it of *yours* whether or not Geoffrey pays off this Quarles female?''

Vivien flushed with anger at this sisterly ingratitude. ''It was you who asked me to involve myself! As your brother, of course I must protect your interests.''

Had she asked Vivien to involve himself? Augusta could not properly recall. ''I have changed my mind!'' she said with dignity. ''I see now that this is something Geoffrey and I must ourselves resolve. Too many cooks spoil the broth! And so I thank you for your efforts, Vivien—though it seems to me you have made things worse instead of better!—and ask that you henceforth refrain." She rose from the couch.

Vivien did not take kindly to this dismissal. "Where the *devil* do you think you're going?" he asked.

Lady Grey opened her eyes wide. "Why, to Geoffrey, of course!"

What the devil was it about Elphinstone that inspired such misplaced loyalty? Exasperated, Vivien grasped his sister's shoulders and forced her to sit down. "You are not," he said very clearly, "to go to Elphinstone! You are not to see him, or to speak with him, or to communicate with him in any manner until this business is done, and perhaps not even then. If you will not be sensible, then I must be sensible for you. Do you understand me, Gus?"

She could hardly fail to do so. Vivien's fingers were digging very uncomfortably into her arms. "Yes, Vivien!" said Gus.

"Good!" He released her and stepped back.

Augusta rubbed her bruised arms. She disliked her brother's expression and the purposeful manner in which he moved toward the door. "Vivien! What are you going to do?" she cried.

"I'm going to see this business resolved one way or another!" On this ominous note, Vivien slammed the door.

Lady Grey breathed a deep sigh of relief. She was not afraid of her brother, but it was exhausting to be around someone in such a dreadful rage. Gracious, but Vivien had been angry! Not since childhood had he treated her that rough way. Augusta recalled how he used to order her about. But they were not children now! How dare he try to tell her what she might and might not do? It was very aggravating. Yes, and so was the odious way in which Vivien spoke of poor Geoffrey, as if he had not more than once blotted his own copybook.

Geoffrey! Augusta blanched as she recalled that she had asked Vivien to call Geoffrey out. She had not meant it, naturally, had spoken out of grief and rage. But such was Vivien's frame of mind—and his parting words could well have been a threat.

Lady Grey sprang to her feet, tugged violently at the bell, ran to the door and flung it open, and dashed out into the hall. "Grimsley! Grimsley!" she called, as she sped up the stairs. Geoffrey must be warned, before it was too late. "Grimsley! Whatever shall I wear?"

Chapter Twenty-one

Ermyntrude sat sulkily on the window seat. As result of her most recent escapade, she had been forbidden to leave the house. Ermyntrude thought it very bad. Finally she had contrived to pique St. Erth's interest, and her pa would not allow her to take advantage of that fact. Perhaps if she asked him once more, ever so prettily, or flung herself upon his mercy and explained that it must be a nunnery for her if she could not have St. Erth— surely Sir Geoffrey could not consign his favorite daughter to such an awful fate. Ermyntrude knew she must be her papa's favorite daughter; who could prefer Drusilla to herself?

Drusilla had been whiling away the time with a desultory game of patience. Now she threw down her cards. "*Where* are Tabby and Lambchop? Tabby should have been back ages ago! Perhaps she sneaked in without us seeing her. I'll just go and see!"

Ermyntrude made no demur. To her sister's restless company, she preferred her own unhappy thoughts. How unkind it was of everyone to interfere with her romance. At this rate, by the time Ermyntrude saw St. Erth again, he would have forgotten her altogether, and she would have to start over again from scratch. But her papa wouldn't let her do so. Ermyntrude saw that she was destined to remain on the shelf. She decided that before she became an ape-leader, she would put a period to her own existence. Then they would all regret that they had not appreciated her more when she was alive, Tabby and her papa and St. Erth. Even Drusilla would be sorry. As for Ermyntrude's various suitors, they must all be cast into the dumps.

Her spirits raised by these reflections, Ermyntrude smoothed the skirt of her fashionable chemise dress, which was made of muslin, fitted to the bosom, with a lace frill round the throat and fluting round the sleeves and hem. Her papa, stricken with remorse, would give her the grandest funeral Brighton had ever seen. She would look especially lovely, her golden hair arranged becomingly, her gown the one Tabby had filched and maligned. Everyone would lament the loss of a maiden so lovely and so young. The gentlemen would flock around the coffin, displaying gratifying grief. St. Erth would realize what ecstasy could have been his—alas, too late. As for poor Osbert, most devoted of her swains—why, he would fling himself upon the coffin and clasp her cold corpse to his breast. Of course, he would never love again, would mourn her all his days, would shudder even to so much as look at another female. Ermyntrude frowned. Perhaps she should leave a list of instructions. It would be just like her family to bury her in the wrong dress.

Drusilla burst into the room then. She held a letter in her hand. "Tabby *has* been here!" she cried. "But she isn't now. This was on her pillow, and all her things are gone!"

"Gone?" Ermyntrude reached out. "Let me see that, Dru!"

Drusilla snatched away the letter. "It's addressed to Pa. We can't go around reading his letters, Ermy! You know we can't."

But Ermyntrude had put two and two together. She abandoned the window seat to chase her sister round the room. "You silly twit! Let me have that letter, do! Who has a better right to read it? 'Twas *my* beau Tabby was making sheep's eyes at!"

Drusilla placed a zebrawood sofa between her sister and herself. "Have you gone off your hinges? Tabby did nothing of the sort!"

"Oh, yes, she did!" Ermyntrude ducked around the sofa and grabbed for the letter. "She was racketing around with Osbert, was she not? For all we know, she may even have set her bonnet at St. Erth. Indeed, I would wager on it! I knew there was something havey-cavey about her ever since she filched my gown!" Drusilla had backed into a corner. Ermyntrude pounced. "Aha!"

Sir Geoffrey paused in the doorway. he was feeling a trifle set-upon in his own right, and had therefore this day repaired to an establishment on the seafront where highly scented steam baths and shampoos were offered as a cure. He had submitted to being steamed till his brains whirled, and then vigorously plummeted and slapped. The treatment had even made him feel a little better, in that it had distracted him from his woes. Unfortunately, those woes were apparently lurking in ambush to beset him the instant he stepped into his house. "What the *deuce* is going on here?" he inquired. "Unhand your sister, Ermyntrude! I thought I told you already that it's not the thing for young women to go about making wagers. And it's definitely not the thing for you to speak unkindly of Tabby. She has tried very hard to do her best for us. If she has not succeeded, it is not her fault, and it is very shabby in you to be so unkind."

Ermyntrude bit her lip in vexation. "Pa, you don't understand. Tabby's taken French leave!"

Sir Geoffrey frowned at his elder daughter toward whom he was beginning to feel something grievously akin to dislike. "Have you been ripping up at her?" he asked. "Because, Ermyntrude, that's not what I can like!"

"Of all the unjust things to say!" Ermyntrude took an agitated turn around the room. "If anyone's been mistreated, it's me, because I'm not allowed out of the house! But since you will not believe me, here!" She thrust Tabby's letter under her papa's nose.

Sir Geoffrey took it with great reluctance. He had developed a strong aversion to letter writing of late. But this was not Mrs. Quarles's handwriting or Augusta's. He opened the epistle and began to read.

Anxiously, Drusilla and Ermyntrude watched their papa, tried without success to read his silently moving lips. "Love letters!" he said aloud. "Surely she wouldn't stoop to that!"

"Love letters!" echoed Ermyntrude. "From whom? Not St. Erth! I tell you, if Tabby has gone off and eloped with St. Erth, I *shall* blow my brains out!"

"That's all fine and good," snapped Drusilla, "but it's *my* dog she took with her! Are you going to tell us what she wrote you, Pa, or not?"

Sir Geoffrey was still struggling with the intimation that Mrs. Quarles had wished to make the whole world privy to the impassioned outpourings of his pen. "The ingratitude!" he said. "What, puss? Oh, the letter! I don't see why you may not read it. Perhaps you may tell me what all this is about!"

Drusilla hoped she might do so. She took the letter from her papa's hand. " 'You and your family have been all kindness, and I have grown attached to you all. I cannot bear that you should set your faces against me, yet know that you must be disappointed and shocked. I most earnestly conjure you to believe that all is not as it seems! You will understand that I have no choice but to leave you. It distresses me beyond measure to take this step; I hesitated in forming my decision, but nothing less will answer the purpose. At least I may assure you that certain letters of a compromising character will not reach the public eye. Mrs. Quarles can no longer threaten you with that. Pray consider this small act a token of my esteem, and believe me your grateful and devoted Tabby.' '' Drusilla finished reading, and let the letter fall.

There was a brief silence in the drawing room, as its various inhabitants sough surreptitiously to dry their eyes. Drusilla was first to recover from the moving letter that she'd just read aloud. "What's set Tabby to acting like a loony, that's what I'd like to know!"

"Tabby?" came a voice from the doorway, and Mr. Philpotts walked into the room. "Forgive me for not having myself announced. There seems to be a bit of a contretemps below stairs." His anxious gaze rested on Ermyntrude. "Some young woman has gone off in a carriage. I thought you had eloped."

"Not me. Tabby!" Ermyntrude collapsed onto the window seat. "The question is, with whom!"

Sir Geoffrey was less concerned with whom than why. "It makes no sense!" said he. "Why should we turn our faces against Tabby? She's quite one of the family!"

"Yes," agreed Drusilla. "If we can put up with Ermyntrude, I don't see why we should cavil at anything Tabby might think of. Except that it was very bad of her to take my dog!"

Mr. Philpotts was in need of further enlightenment. He picked up the letter that Drusilla had let fall. Under more ordinary circumstances he would not have made so bold as to read it, but he was concerned. "Ah!" he said, upon scanning the letter's contents. "I see! Miss Minchin fears she has sullied her reputation and does not wish to involve you in any notoriety—even thought it was on your behalf that she did so, Ermy! And so you meant her to, when you set out to compromise St. Erth. But what is this about love letters? I don't understand.''

Suddenly, Drusilla did. "Tabby pinched them!" she cried. "She must have snuck them right out from under that female's nose! Good for her! But how could she think we could condemn her, after that? She didn't need to run away!''

"If she *did* run away!" said Ermyntrude, despondent to think that her most devoted suitor had just read her a scold. "Perhaps it had nothing to do with us at all. Perhaps"— she looked wise—"an unhappy love affair!''

Drusilla and Sir Geoffrey both thought of a certain recent conversation concerning Lady Grey's rakehell brother. "Ah!" They sighed. Then Sir Geoffrey frowned. "But she said she'd sullied her reputation. If that reprobate has trifled with Tabby, damned if I shan't call him out!''

Osbert interrupted these speculations. "Do you mean to let Miss Minchin go?''

"Let her go?" echoed Sir Geoffrey, with a wistful thought of how smoothly, under Tabby's guidance, his household had run. "Of course not! That is, we wouldn't if she'd given us a choice. Poor puss, all alone in the world—yes, and without a penny, because I forgot to pay her her wage!''

"Pa!" Ermyntrude's excellent imagination was at work. "All manner of terrible things might happen to her! We must get her back!''

"Yes!" added Drusilla. "And Lambchop!''

"She can't have gone far without money," said Sir Geoffrey. "Perhaps if we were to instigate a search—''

Osbert cleared his throat. "I believe your servants may know something about the business. There was a discussion to that effect underway when I arrived at your front door.''

Sir Geoffrey was not slow to act on this suggestion.

Within moments an unhappy-looking footman was undergoing an inquisition in the drawing room. "How was I to know anything was amiss?" he protested. "It's not for me to tell the family they may not go out!"

Sir Geoffrey sought to soothe the footman's wounded feelings. "I'm sure you did just what you ought! What *did* you do, by the way?"

The footman had done precious little, it turned out— save to carry Tabby's shabby portmanteau out to a waiting carriage. But his audience was clearly disappointed by this admission, and he elaborated on his tale. "There was a gentleman waiting within," he added, with the satisfaction of one who knows he has dropped a bombshell.

"A gentleman!" Ermyntrude so far forgot herself as to grasp the footman and give him a good shake. "What did he look like?"

"A gentleman!" responded the poor footman, taken quite aback by this familiarity. "I didn't get a good look at him, Miss Ermyntrude! But I did hear him say as he would take her to London!"

"London!" Ermyntrude released the footman. "I was right; she did elope!"

"Adone-do!" said Sir Geoffrey impatiently. "You have elopements on the brain. I read her letter; it's clear as anything that she's run away. And if she had a friend to help her, so much the better, because there is less chance that she may come to harm." He glowered at the footman. "How long ago was this, man?"

The footman felt absurdly guilty. "Why, sir, not an hour past."

"An hour!" Sir Geoffrey brightened. Perhaps chaos might still be held at bay. "We may still catch up with them on the London road and coax her to come home."

"We'll take my carriage! My team's already harnessed!" Osbert followed Sir Geoffrey into the hall. Left

172

alone with the footman, Ermyntrude and Drusilla exchanged glances. "*Damned* if I'll be left behind!" cried Ermyntrude; whereupon the young ladies dashed together through the door.

Chapter Twenty-two

Elphinstone House had not seen the end of contretemps yet this day. Next to arrive on the front doorstep was Lady Grey. She was not so haggard as she thought herself, although her green eyes had lost some of their sparkle and her chestnut hair its sheen. No similar fault could be found in her costume: sprigged muslin walking dress; pelisse, open on the side and trimmed with lace; conversation bonnet, kid gloves, pretty boots. Her driver assisted her to alight from her carriage. She reached into her large lozenge-shaped reticule and drew out her vinaigrette. Then she squared her shoulders and set out up the front walk.

"You are surprised to see me here, Geoffrey!" she said in none-too-steady tones. "Yes, and so you should be! You *do* deserve to be condemned for your conduct; you should have known better than to do what you did! I cannot describe to you the way I felt when I read that woman's note, realized that she had given you—" Gus had recourse to her vinaigrette. "The suggestion was enough to bring on one of my bad turns! I tried very hard to set my face most sternly against you, Geoffrey! I was distressed beyond measure—I felt as though my heart must break!"

Sir Geoffrey's footman was also distressed. Not only had he endured a rare trimming from Sir Geoffrey's superior valet, Sir Geoffrey had also called him to task. Now here was Lady Grey on the doorstep, talking to herself. It was all most disconcerting. But a good footman did not react to the vagaries of his superiors. "The family," he said woodenly, "is not at home."

"Oh!" Gus had not considered that her errand might be for naught. "Where have they gone? It is imperative that I speak with Sir Geoffrey without delay!"

"As to that, milady—" With a startled expression, the footman broke off. Lady Grey turned, impatient to know what the man was goggling at. Then she also stared.

A woman was coming up the sidewalk. Certainly she was worthy of anyone's attention in her military-style cherry spencer and her pink-striped neck scarf; her pretty muslin walking dress worn over a yellow slip and her yellow boots. But it was not the woman's costume that had caught the attention of her audience. "Lawks!" said the footman unenthusiastically. " 'Tis Miss Drusilla's hound!"

"So it is," agreed Margot, as she and Lambchop came to a panting halt. "And he has very nearly pulled my arm from its socket in her eagerness to be home. My larder, you see, he has already cleaned out! Do take the leash while I have a word with your master, there's a good fellow!"

The footman would have liked to have so pretty a lady think well of him; unfortunately, it was not to be. For one thing, as he had already told the other lady, Sir Geoffrey was not in. For another, he had refused to have anything to do with Lambchop since the beast had bitten him, despite the assurances of the entire household that it had been meant in fun. As he explained these things, the footman fell back several paces. Lambchop collapsed across the threshold and wagged his tail.

"Not at home!" echoed Margot. "Now here's a pretty pass. Perhaps you might tell me where he's taken himself to, because it is very important that I speak with him before much more time has passed."

Lady Grey stirred. "I thought you looked familiar! Now I realize it is the hat. How *dare* you come here and brazenly demand to see Geoffrey?"

Quizzically, Margot regarded her fellow visitor. "My hat? Have you one like it, then? I shall be very angry in that case, because my milliner assured me it was one of a kind."

"No, I haven't one like it!" Gus looked very haughty. "Not would I wish to, because I consider it the most vulgar hat I have ever seen! You do not recognize me? Allow me to refresh your memory! I was with Geoffrey on the esplanade when you sent him that note—Mrs. Quarles!"

"I sent Geoffrey *several* notes!" contered Margot, and smiled. "To not a one of which did he deign to reply. You are Lady Grey, of course. I must felicitate you for having brought Geoffrey up to scratch."

"Thank you!" Gus returned the smile with what she fancied an equal insincerity. "I shall take care he doesn't wriggle off my hook despite *your* best efforts to the contrary!"

"My best efforts?" Margot opened her eyes wide. "You mistake the matter. I don't want Geoffrey back. He is much better off leg-shackled to you! I was just a passing fancy, while *you* have obviously sent the poor man tumbling head over heels!"

Had she done so? Gus could not help but be gratified. "Do you really think so?" she inquired.

"Anyone must think so!" Margot responded cheerfully. "Geoffrey is to be congratulated on his good sense. The pair of you will run on very well together, and you may take my word on that, for I have had some small experience in such things."

From all accounts, Mrs. Quarles's experience was not small. "If you think so highly of Geoffrey, you have a strange way of showing it!'' retorted Gus. ''I am aware of your evil designs, Mrs. Quarles! I suppose you mean to create more food for scandal by coming to this house!''

Margot had meant no such thing. Her designs, in this instance, had been selfless; she had wished to know what Sir Geoffrey had to do with her daughter. For this tardy maternal concern to be so grossly misunderstood made her very cross. ''*I*'m not the one who's providing grist for the gossip mongers' mills! *You* are the one who wishes to brangle, whereas I am merely doing what I must.''

''Indeed?'' Lady Grey arched her brows. ''You find that you must bring unhappiness into so many lives? Rather than what you must, Mrs. Quarles, you do what you can!''

Made even more cross by this unkind allegation, Margot stamped her foot. Prudently, Lambchop moved out of harm's way. ''What would *you* know about it?'' Margot responded. ''You who have never dared defy the laws of propriety to follow the dictates of your heart? You tempt the gods themselves with your arrogance. Beware! One can never be certain of what lengths one may be drawn into, and you may take my word on that!''

Lady Grey was stung by the inference that she lacked courage. ''I am not so starched-up as you seem to think!'' she cried. ''*Not* that you make a case for freedom from the shackles that hamper a respectable lady! Rather, you seem to be quite incapable of handling your own affairs!''

There was some truth in this allegation. That fact did not endear its utterer to Margot. ''I shan't allow you to get a rise out of me!'' she said. ''*That* would be a choice item of tittle-tattle—the pair of us on Geoffrey's doorstep, at daggers drawn.''

But that is precisely what they were. The fascinated footman stirred. He'd be blamed for this upset also, he supposed, even though he didn't know what he could have done to prevent it taking place. He didn't know what he might do now, except to suggest that the ladies might wish to repair to the drawing room.

"What an excellent notion!" said Margot, at the very same instant Lady Grey said, "No!" Margot regarded her quizzically. "Only over my dead body," Gus said grimly, "will you set foot across this threshold!"

"Over your—" Margot arched her brows. "High flights, ma'am!"

She took a step forward. Augusta grasped her arm. The ladies struggled in a genteel manner, while the horrified footman begged that they would not.

No one could explain later what next transpired. One theory was that Lambchop had grown bored and deemed it time again to indulge in play. Another argued that Lady Grey's half-hysterical manner roused some sympathetic chord in his canine heart. At all event he raised up on his back legs, placed his great paws on Gus's shoulders, and gave her face a lick. Gus did not respond favorably to this friendly interest. She screamed. That scream inspired Lambchop to further efforts to ingratiate himself. So energetic was the dog in his caress that he knocked Lady Grey right off her feet.

"Good God!" cried Margot, and grabbed at Lambchop's collar, while the footman scrambled to retrieve Gus's vinaigrette. "Get off her, you wretched brute!" The hound recognized the voice of authority. He sat down.

It was at this moment that Mr. Sanders arrived on the scene, to discover a melee under way at Sir Geoffrey's front door. So very startling was the scene that, despite his excessively bad temper, he stopped for a moment to stare. Then he recognized the shaggy beast perched athwart his fallen sister as the same hound that had recently attempted to savage both Perry and himself; and also the female who was pulling at its collar and swearing like a trooper, to no avail.

Vivien swore also, as he set out up the walk. His approach to the problem was more direct: He lifted the hound bodily in his arms and set it aside. Then he thrust the leash at Margot. "See if you can't control your cursed dog!"

Margot did not bother to explain that Lambchop did not belong to her. She watched as Vivien pushed aside the footman, who had been attempting to revive Lady Grey with her vinaigrette, and pulled his sister roughly to her feet. "I thought I told you that you were not to come here!" he growled. "You may imagine my dismay when I called at your house and Grimsley told me where you'd gone. Can I not leave you alone for a moment, Gus?"

Lady Grey wished her brother would leave her alone for several moments while she recovered from what had surely been a close brush with death. "Don't scold me!" she whimpered. "You perceive that it is imperative I speak with Geoffrey!"

Margot could not help but feel sorry for Lady Grey, so disheveled and so pale. "I was right," she commented. "You *are* an ill-tempered brute, sir! Why shouldn't your sister speak with Geoffrey if she wishes without asking your say-so? After all, they are betrothed!"

Vivien turned angrily to her. "Ma'am, you try my civility too high! But since you will have the truth, I've no wish to see my sister hobnobbing with females of your sort."

Lady Grey found herself in the strange position of rebelliously wishing to defend Mrs. Quarles. "I cannot think that this is a proper conversation!" she said. "And when it comes down to it, Vivien, it is not kind of you to speak so to Mrs. Quarles, when you have spent a number of years hobnobbing with females of *just* her sort!"

Mr. Sanders looked even more furious. Margot smiled. "Don't put yourself in a pucker on my account, Lady Grey! The truth of the matter is that Mr. Sanders has the wrong sow by the ear. But we musn't quarrel. We're here

179

for the same purpose, are we not? To speak with Geoffrey!''

Vivien had an unpleasant suspicion that he was not showing to advantage in this exchange. "Where *is* Elphinstone?" he snapped, in an attempt to regain control. "I've a few words to say to him on my own account."

The footman had withdrawn again into the hallway, where several of his fellow servants had also been drawn by the commotion. "The family," he repeated, "is not at home."

"So you said before!" Margot awarded the man her most dazzling smile. "How very inconvenient! Where do you think they might have gone?"

This question the footman could answer. "London! Alongside of Miss Tabby—an elopement, by all accounts!"

Margot was stunned by the implications of this statement. "Lud!" she breathed.

"An elopement!" wailed Lady Grey.

"How *could* he?" Vivien growled. "Who the devil is 'Miss Tabby'?"

Margot took firmer grip on Lambchop, who showed signs of reawakening energy. "You will recall the young woman whom you mistook for me," she said.

Vivien did, indeed. "Your sister?" he said slowly.

"Your *sister*?" echoed Lady Grey, horrified.

Margot could hardly blame her. "It is not as it appears. We have been estranged. Tabby's relationship with Sir Geoffrey has only recently become know to me."

Tabby. The little governess. Did Geoffrey's perfidy know no limits? Gus tottered toward Margot. "He has played us both false, the fiend!"

"Apparently so." Margot was hard-pressed to keep her balance, with Lady Grey clutching at her one arm and Lambchop hanging on the other, straining at his leash. "It would seem we have both been misled."

Vivien thought the woman singularly cold hearted. "Yes, and so will your sister be!" he pointed out. "Or is the estrangement between you so great that you do not care for that, Mrs. Quarles?"

The man chided her for lack of family feeling? Margot supposed she deserved his scorn. "I care a great deal, Mr. Sanders!" she retorted. "I would not wish my poor Tabby to be mistreated by anyone. Indeed, I feel very keenly that I must be partially to blame for this dreadful occurrence. Due to my neglect, Tabby has little knowledge of the world."

Lady Grey was touched by this obvious sincerity. To think she had once been jealous of the young woman who even now was teetering on the brink of ruin. "We must not allow Geoffrey to do this dreadful thing!" she cried.

So his Miss Nevermind was an innocent, after all? Vivien felt a surge of renewed hope. Then he recalled that innocents didn't generally elope. There seemed only one way to find out what was true and what was not. He strode briskly down the walk toward his waiting cabriolet.

Gus stared after him "Vivien? Where are you going?"

"To settle this business!" Mr. Sanders responded grimly. "Once and for all!" He flung himself into the cabriolet and set off down the street.

Lady Grey took no comfort from her brother's prospective intervention in the elopement. "Poor Geoffrey!" she wailed. "I know I should not think kindly of him after all he has done to us, but I cannot help but be concerned, Mrs. Quarles! Vivien has a dreadful temper, and if he should encounter Geoffrey now, I dread to think what will be the outcome. Perhaps they may even kill each other— or worse!"

Margot could only agree with these apprehensions. Additionally, she was concerned with Tabby's welfare. Margot was startled to realize that she was even more concerned about Tabby than her post-obit bills.

181

If this was what it was like to be a parent, Margot was glad she'd come to it so late. Her anxious gaze alighted upon Lady Grey's carriage. "Ha!" she said.

Lady Grey recognized that her companion had had a brainstorm. She, too, gazed at the waiting vehicle. "Oho!" she agreed. Within seconds, Margot and Gus and Lambchop were setting out on the trail of Vivien's cabriolet.

Chapter Twenty-three

Tabby winced as she stubbed her toe against a pebble in the dusty road. Perry, following behind her, took this expression of dismay as a personal comment. "You may blame yourself, you know!" he snapped, as he sought a more comfortable grip on her shabby portmanteau. "You were the one as *would* wish to go to London, though dashed if I know why! It ain't at all the place for a girl like you. It wouldn't even be the place for you if you was what Viv said, which I didn't believe for more than a moment, which is why I waited to speak with you after Viv had gone off!" He readjusted the portmanteau. "Which I don't mind admitting to you, I wish I hadn't done!"

Tabby could not blame him for this feeling. She, too, wished she'd had some other choice. "Mrs. Phipps is in London," she explained, not for the first time. "My uncle's housekeeper. She is living with her sister. I'm sure they'll take me in until I decide what I am to do."

Perry stubbed his own toe then and swore. "Dashed if I don't see why you couldn't have stayed where you was! Instead of talking *me* into wasting the ready on a hired hack that wouldn't stand the pace! Now here we are stuck out in the middle of nowhere with a broken axle that must be repaired!"

Tabby refrained from pointing out that the axle had been

broken as result of Perry's wishing to demonstrate himself a notable whip. All she had asked was that he buy her a seat on the stage. But Perry had been shocked at the suggestion that she should undertake such a journey alone. And so here they were. "You know perfectly well that I could not stay with Sir Geoffrey!" she said. "Not with Margot threatening him with blackmail. And I could hardly apply to her for refuge, after I had stolen her letters so she couldn't blackmail him. Look, Perry! I thought this section of the road looked familiar. There is the inn where we first met!"

Perry brightened, not because he recalled that occasion with any pleasure, but at the memory of the excellent quality of the innkeeper's ale. His pace quickened. Within moments, they had reached the inn. The innkeeper met them in the doorway. He scowled at sight of these new guests. "You!" he said to Tabby, recalling a great ruckus in the middle of the night. "It's that sorry I am to tell you I haven't a room left!"

"No need to be sorry!" Perry wondered why Tabby's cheeks had turned so pink. "We don't want a room, just a spot of something to eat and a drop of ale. Just bring it out here to the picnic table!" Perry heaved the portmanteau onto the wooden table and collapsed upon a bench.

Tabby was less quick to follow, stared up at the inn. Behind which window lay the room where she and Vivien first met? She could not tell. Now she would not meet him again, ever. The thought made her very sad. Tabby told herself it was for the best as she sat down on the wooden bench.

Perry could not help but realize his companion was not in the best of spirits. He could not blame her for it, though his own spirits were improving with each sip of the innkeeper's excellent ale. "Dashed if it ain't that same rooster!" he said, as the russet fowl poked an inquisitive head

184

around the base of the gnarled oak. Tabby smiled wanly and crumbled a muffin for the bird to eat.

Some moments passed in this fashion, as the travelers took their ease. The warmth of the sun was soothing, as were the country sounds, even the occasional distant clatter of traffic on the road. Tabby began to feel peaceful. Perry, with the additional inducement of consumed ale, drowsily closed his eyes.

The peace was shattered by a female voice. "There she is!" it cried. "I told you she had eloped!" Perry leaped up to find himself confronted by a wrathful vision, which stared at him in confusion. "Gracious! Who are *you*?"

Tabby had jumped also, knocking the plate of muffins to the ground to the delight of the russet rooster, which promptly began to feast. "Ermyntrude!" gasped Tabby. "Whatever are you doing here?" Then she realized that Drusilla was also present, and Sir Geoffrey and Mr. Philpotts.

Sir Geoffrey took her hand. "M'dear, we couldn't let you run off like that! Whatever nonsensical notion you may have taken into your head about sinking yourself quite below reproach. Which I don't know how you could, considering that you've saved us from the clutches of that female."

Tabby was touched by this kindness. "I cannot take advantage of you, sir!" she replied gruffly. "You see, Mrs. Quarles—"

Mr. Philpotts cleared his throat. "If I may interrupt—I fancy I understand your motives, Miss Minchin! And applaud you for them as well. You appreciate the delicacy of your position and fear that you will be looked upon as a person not fit for association with respectable people. You realize everyone must see your conduct in the most unfavorable light. *I* know your motives were the purest, but the way of the world is such that others will not credit your selflessness. I should have tried harder to dissuade you and feel very badly that I did not. I wish you will let me make it up to you. Give up this foolish journey and return to London as my wife.''

A brief silence followed this startling proposal. Not Tabby alone was stunned. Ermyntrude thought at first that Osbert was practicing making her his offer. She must tell him that a great deal more ardor was required and considerably less melancholy tones. Not that she could seriously consider his suit; her heart belonged to St. Erth.

Tabby interrupted Ermyntrude's reflections. "Stuff!" she said. "You are making a great piece of work about nothing. As for your kind offer, I am very grateful to you for it, but you must see that it is impossible!"

He had not been practicing! Ermyntrude had expected Osbert to fling himself upon her coffin, and consequently felt betrayed. "If this don't beat all!" she cried. "I am shocked, Osbert, that you would play fast and loose with me. It *is* me you was professing to be mad for, was it not, just the other day? As for you *you*—" she glared at Tabby. "So this is how you go on behind my back, you—you Jezebel! By inviting my suitors to make you the object of their gallantry.''

Osbert turned toward Ermyntrude. He was pale. "I didn't—

She cut him off. "I hope you will both be very happy! The pair of you deserve the other!" Ermyntrude turned and with immense dignity walked away. Behind her, she heard Osbert groan. This small satisfaction was marred by Tabby's next remark. "Let her go," said that traitress. "There's no reasoning with her when she's on her high ropes."

Ermyntrude swept around the side of the building, cheeks aflame. How dared Tabby speak of her in that disrespectful manner, Tabby who was a mere employee in Ermyntrude's own house? Blinded by her rage, Ermyntrude did not look where she was going. In the next instant, she bumped against a masculine chest.

The gentleman grasped her arm to prevent a ñasty fall. "Oh!" said Ermyntrude, and glanced up to find herself in the possession of no less than St. Erth. He did not look glad to see her. Ermyntrude recalled that she had meant to impress him with her delicacy. Not a lass to miss an opportunity, she swooned.

St. Erth did not let her fall, of course; but he slung her unromantically over his shoulder, rather as if she were a sack of meal. He then carried her around the corner of the building and deposited her ungently on the picnic table. "I thought I heard your daughter's voice!" he cried to Sir Geoffrey. "Surely it was not with your connivance that she followed me here! I do not scruple to tell you that she is the most pushing, rag-mannered, cursedly *aggravating* piece of business I have ever met!" He scowled at the recumbent Ermyntrude. "Rather than bed her, I would prefer to remain celibate for the remainder of my days!"

Sir Geoffrey also regarded his daughter. "I can understand how you might feel that way!" he said. "The thing is, we didn't follow you here. It was Tabby here who—" He realized the imprudence of acquainting St. Erth with the truth. "Who thought this a splendid day for a jaunt!"

St. Erth scowled at Tabby. "You were in on it, too, were you? Again?"

"No, sir, I was not!" Tabby couldn't blame the viscount for his suspicions, but wished that Ermyntrude were conscious to see him display himself in so unfavorable a light. "I assure you, sir, that we did not know you would be here today."

"Perhaps not." St. Erth was obliged to concede that he didn't know how anyone could have anticipated his movements. He glared at Ermyntrude. "But I wouldn't put anything past the little jade!"

"Little jade!" echoed Osbert, who was white with

rage. "How dare you speak so, St. Erth? Perhaps Miss Elphinstone has been a trifle imprudent, but her recklessness stemmed only from a genuine devotion to you. Ermy is little more than a child, after all!"

"Ermy, is it?" sneered the viscount. "What other familiarities has she accorded you, Philpotts? Bad enough the chit is as bold as a brass-faced monkey. Now it also seems she may well be spoiled goods!"

This insult was too great for anyone to swallow, save Drusilla, who had gone to look about for her missing pet and therefore did not hear. "Sir!" gasped Tabby, even as Sir Geoffrey cried, "I say!" Ermyntrude sat up, pink with indignation, and Perry wished himself miles away. But it was Osbert who took action. He drew back his fist and drove it into the viscount's face.

"Planted him a facer!" remarked Perry, in case anyone had failed to notice. "And drew his cork as well!"

Ermyntrude watched with satisfaction as St. Erth fumbled for handkerchief with which to staunch the blood flowing from his nose. "Oh, Osbert!" she breathed. "That was very brave! How foolish I am. I did not realize the sort of man St. Erth is! The scales have quite fallen from my eyes."

"Thank God!" muttered the viscount into his bloody handkerchief.

Ermyntrude ignored this untimely interruption. She gazed soulfully at Osbert and sighed. "How very brave you were! Because now, of course, St. Erth will call you out!"

Sir Geoffrey deemed it time to exercise parental authority. "Oh, no, St. Erth will not! There'll be no duels fought over you, miss!" he decreed. "Gus was right; you have been allowed to run wild! It's time someone took you in hand."

Took her in hand? This was very bad. Ermyntrude glanced at Osbert for support. Mr. Philpotts, however, had turned back to Tabby. "Pray reconsider my offer," he said. "Allow me to protect you from slanders such as these. I know you do not love me—I do not expect it— nor will I insult you by saying you have taken my fancy to an alarming degree. More important, I believe we would deal well together, Miss Minchin. And I would do my utmost to make you happy."

Ermyntrude could not believe what she was hearing. "Tabby! You aren't going to accept? If you do, I'll never speak to you again!"

Sir Geoffrey wished, in a somewhat unpaternal manner, that his elder daughter might succumb to another swoon. "Hush, puss! Tabby must do as she thinks best." He glanced at Perry. "Unless it's true that she's already eloping with someone else!"

"No, no!" gasped Tabby, as Perry chocked on the remainder of his ale. "Perry is an old friend, who was kind enough to bear me company on my trip."

"Thereby compromising you!" Osbert said sternly. "You must curb this tendency toward unconventional behavior, Miss Minchin, or you will truly find yourself in the suds. I beg you to reconsider. As my wife—"

"No!" Ermyntrude leaped up from the picnic table and clutched Osbert's arm. "She shan't have you! I know I've been very foolish, but in my heart I've always been yours!" Osbert stared at her, clearly at a loss for words. Viscount St. Erth, who had been trying to determine whether or not a duel was called for, so much enjoyed the sight of Mr. Philpotts's discomfiture that he sat down beside Perry, prepared to be further entertained.

Sir Geoffrey was more concerned with Tabby. "What you didn't say was why you thought you must go away! I thought you was happy with us, puss! We thought you quite one of the family, you know."

Tabby could not bear to think she'd hurt her kindly em-

189

ployer's feelings. "I *was* happy! You don't understand. Mrs. Quarles—"

"The devil with Mrs. Quarles!" said Sir Geoffrey. "She's no threat to us now—and for that, m'dear, we're in your debt. Allow us to repay you! Come along now and forget this nonsense!"

"Yes, but she's not to marry Osbert!" put in Ermyntrude, taking firmer grip on her bemused swain. "Pa, say she's not!"

"Tabby will marry whomever she wishes!" Sir Geoffrey frowned at his daughter. "To my way of thinking, Philpotts would do better to have her than you!"

"Yes, but he shan't!" said Tabby, before Ermyntrude could erupt into further protest. "I very solemnly assure you that I don't wish to marry anyone!"

"Then that's settled!" Ermyntrude sighed. A dreadful thought struck her. "Osbert, you don't *mind*?"

Mind that the seemingly unattainable object of his affections was snuggled in his arms? Osbert thought not. But Ermyntrude must learn that he would not dwell under the hen's foot. "Well," he said, "we'll see!"

"Good!" said Sir Geoffrey, in response not to Mr. Philpotts but to Tabby's disavowal of any matrimonial plans. "Then Tabby may come along home with me!"

Tabby wished she might. She regarded Sir Geoffrey's hand. Before she could shatter his hopes, Perry started as if he'd seen a ghost. "Viv!"

Vivien Sanders had indeed come round the corner of the inn some moments past, had stood observing the group gathered around the rustic little table set beneath the gnarled oak. What he had just witnessed had in no way altered certain notions that he'd taken into his mind. He had not expected to discover that Perry was a traitor, true; but Perry's perfidy could be dealt with at another time. He strode toward the table until he was face-to-face with the gentleman who had just made Tabby an improper offer. "Elphinstone?" he asked.

Sir Geoffrey had no idea who this angry-looking stranger was. Yes, and he felt a little angry himself at being interrupted in the midst of his impassioned plea. "Yes, I'm Elphinstone!" he retorted. "What of it? Who the deuce are you, and what do you want?"

Vivien allowed his actions to speak for him. He stripped off his glove and slapped Sir Geoffrey across the cheek.

Drusilla came around the table. "Tabby! What have you done with Lambchop?" she cried. Then she became aware of the shocked silence. Tabby, for all her fits and starts, still seemed the most sensible person present now that Ermyntrude had Mr. Philpotts acting like a mooncalf. Drusilla hurried to Tabby's side. "What's happened, Tabby? What's amiss?"

Tabby reached out, drew Drusilla closer. "I'm afraid," she said faintly, "that Mr. Sanders has just challenged your papa to a duel!"

Chapter Twenty-four

A spirited discussion then evolved, concerning the finer points of etiquette involved in the fighting of a duel. Such was Mr. Sanders's temper that he wished the event to take place immediately. Sir Geoffrey, on his mettle, was inclined to agree. Mr. Philpotts, however, gave it as his opinion that to act so precipitously was not at all the thing. Seconds must be chosen, and certain important points settled, such as weapons, place, and time—that is, if the seconds could not effect a reconciliation, as they were required to try.

"Reconciliation! Never!" A muscle clenched in Vivien's jaw. "Perry! You'll stand up for me."

Perry squirmed. "Glad to, Viv! Thing is, old fellow, wouldn't do you much good! Can't stand the sight of blood—invariably cast up my accounts!"

"Never mind!" put in St. Erth, who was finding the proceedings as entertaining as a play. "I'll stand up for you, Sanders. And Philpotts here can second Elphinstone!"

"Very well!" said Osbert sternly. "But you must swear to utter no more slanders about Ermyntrude!"

The viscount gingerly touched his injured nose. "I'll never so much as say her name again. You have my word on it, Philpotts!"

Ermyntrude had been eyeing Mr. Sanders with interest. So this was Tabby's rakehell. "Oh!" she cried, at the realization that she was to be parted from her newly discovered true love, females having no place on the field of honor, as everyone knew. "This is very bad of you, Pa! You wouldn't allow a duel to be fought over me, and now here you are dueling yourself!"

So, apparently, he was. Sir Geoffrey was not entirely certain how this circumstance had come about. Nor, it appeared, were any of the other parties to the business. Mr. Philpotts and Viscount St. Erth were finding it difficult to agree on who had given the first offense. Granted, Mr. Sanders had struck Sir Geoffrey, which was a grave matter; a blow was strictly prohibited under any circumstances among gentlemen, and no verbal apology could be acceptable for such an insult. Still, one could not but think he'd had some cause.

Mr. Sanders offered them no enlightenment, but spoke scornfully to Perry. "So you are off to butter up your wealthy aunt. How right you were not to let *my* petty business interfere!"

Perry flushed as this barbed comment found its mark. "Dash it, Viv!" he cried. "I think you must have a head full of bees. First you accuse poor Tabby of being no better than she should be, which I knew she couldn't be on account of being old Tolly's niece, and not *this*!"

Mr. Sanders's brows drew together. "And who was old Tolly?" he inquired.

It wasn't often that Perry had the opportunity to put his friend out of countenance. Savoring the moment, he brushed muffin crumbs from his spotted sleeve. Impatiently, Vivien closed his fingers around that same sleeve. "My tutor at Cambridge!" Perry said hastily.

Vivien glanced at Tabby, who was seated on a wooden bench, with Ermyntrude and Drusilla on either side. She was very pale. But he had known she was very fond of

Elphinstone; had she not said so all along? Vivien supposed he would have to refrain from damaging the cad too badly, for her sake.

Mr. Philpotts and St. Erth were making some small progress, having decided that since Lady Grey was Mr. Sanders's sister, then he must have challenged Sir Geoffrey to a duel on her behalf. This was a grave matter, indeed. Any insult to a lady under a gentlemen's care or protection was considered a greater offense than if given to the gentleman directly. "Yes," Osbert said judiciously, "but can Lady Grey be considered to be under Mr. Sanders's care?" The viscount considered and allowed himself uncertain on that point. "But," he added, "offenses originating from the support of a lady's reputation must be considered less justifiable than any other kind!"

Vivien had little patience with this business of seconds. "Confound it!" he said. "This has nothing to do with Gus."

Sir Geoffrey looked bewildered. "No? The devil, man! Then what do you mean by—"

But Gus herself came running around the side of the building then. "Geoffrey! You are surprised to see me here! Yes, and so you should be!" She realized that she had interrupted a tense moment and paused to hear Mr. Philpotts and the viscount discussing the merits of Joe Manton's dueling pistols, which boasted such refinements as a hydraulic barrel tester, a trigger spring, and a fast-firing breech.

"No!" cried Gus, and flung herself between Sir Geoffrey and Vivien. "I did not mean it, Vivien! You must not call him out!" Mr. Philpotts and St. Erth exchanged meaningful glances. Decision making was a thirsty business, even without interruptions by hysterical females. The gentlemen, along with Perry, withdrew to the taproom to refresh themselves with ale.

Lady Grey clutched Sir Geoffrey's jacket. "I was very
194

angry with you, Geoffrey! So angry that I could not even sleep. Each time I closed my eyes, I found myself imagining the most distressing things.''

Sir Geoffrey was also distressed to see his Gus in such a taking. And he could not help but be encouraged by the sight. ''M'dear!'' he said hopefully.

Lady Grey held up a trembling hand. ''No, don't interrupt! I am determined to have my say. I tried very hard to set my face most sternly against you—I felt my heart must break! All the same, I could not believe that you were *truly* a philanderer.'' She gazed up at him beseechingly. ''Pray tell me that you are not, Geoffrey! Of course, it was very foolish of me to think you had remained, er, faithful all these years to the memory of your poor dead wife. I had even determined to overlook your acquaintance with Mrs. Quarles—that is, if you were not betrothed to *me* at the same time you knew her!''

''Betrothed to—'' Sir Geoffrey turned pale at this monstrous suggestion. ''Zounds, Gus! Of course I was not!''

Lady Grey sighed with relief. ''I knew you could not have been, once I thought the matter through. You may be a trifle undisciplined, Geoffrey, but I could not believe you an out-and-out rogue. I cannot claim I do not care about the scandal, because I do, but I am not a coward, no matter what anyone may say. That is, unless—Geoffrey, *did* you seduce that poor child?''

Sir Geoffrey was suffering an understandable confusion. ''*What* child?'' he asked.

''Your Miss Minchin.'' Gus sniffled and fixed her gaze on Sir Geoffrey's cravat. ''Vivien said—''

''Ha!'' interrupted Sir Geoffrey, incensed. ''He did, did he? I should call *him* out, for trifling with our Tabby and making her so unhappy that she had to run away and then trying to pin the blame on me!''

Gus stared at her brother, who was following this exchange with a somewhat glazed expression. ''*Did* he?''

Poor Tabby was mortified. "Oh, no!" she gasped. "It wasn't that at all!"

Lady Grey frowned. "Is that Miss Minchin? Why did she come to talk to me? I don't understand!"

Neither did several of the other people present. Fortunately Lambchop came upon the scene then, with Margot in tow, so startling the russet rooster that had been gorging on muffin crumbs that it jumped into Tabby's lap. "Lambchop!" cried Drusilla, and rushed to greet her pet.

Margot gladly gave the hound over into her keeping. "Now what's this? I could not help but hear—Tabby, just why *are* you here?"

"There you are!" cried Lady Grey. "You're not going to publish, are you, Mrs. Quarles?"

Sir Geoffrey made haste to reassure his Gus. "She can't!" said he.

Margot contemplated her onetime admirer. "Well, Geoffrey. You have certainly played least-in-sight. Why can't I publish, pray?"

Tabby sought to calm the frightened rooster. "I took your letters. It seemed the only way to prevent you from making Sir Geoffrey even more unhappy."

Margot frowned. How sharper than the serpent's tooth— It seemed to her that she was experiencing the full gamut of parental frustrations in a very short time. "I had not even missed the letters. You gave them to Geoffrey, I suppose."

"Certainly I did not!" protested Tabby. The rooster pecked her, and she set him down. "That would have been disloyal to you. I burned them instead."

His spirits considerably revived by the innkeeper's good ale, Perry had strolled back outside. "So she did!" he vouchsafed. "Saw her myself. Still have the stench of that perfumed paper in my nose."

"It is just as well," said Margot. "I didn't truly wish

to publish, at all events. Indeed, Geoffrey, all I wished in the first place was to ask your advice!''

''No harm?'' Sir Geoffrey goggled. ''But you said—''

''I said I wished to speak with you on a matter of personal business, which I did. But that is all I wished until you gave me the cut direct, and then I wished to have revenge. Lud, Geoffrey! If you had thought about it, you would realize I could stand the scandal even less than you.'' Having disposed of Sir Geoffrey to her satisfaction, and additionally made Augusta very curious, Margot turned to Perry. ''You saw Tabby burn the letters? She was traveling with you, then, and not Geoffrey.''

''Not an elopement!'' Perry said quickly. ''Just doing a favor for a friend. And I don't scruple to tell you that it'll be many a long day before I play the Good Samaritan again!''

Augusta noticed Perry then. ''Gracious, Perry, what is that you've got on? You look like a giraffe!''

Perry flushed. ''Dash it, Gus, that's no way to talk to a fellow who's done his best to save your bacon—yes, and so I did, because here you are!''

So she was. Augusta looked mistily up at her fiancé. ''Geoffrey, do you think we might go somewhere else? I wish to speak privately with you.''

Sir Geoffrey would have like nothing better. It was with reluctance that he reminded Lady Grey that he was engaged with her brother to fight a duel.

Ermyntrude was growing restless. She rose from the bench and subjected Vivien to a closer inspection still. ''So you are Tabby's rakehell! Well, you may not have her because she is coming home with us. *I* am going to be married, but Drusilla still needs a governess.''

''I do not need a governess!'' retorted Drusilla, breaking off from reassuring the crestfallen Perry that he did indeed look quite top of the trees. ''I am quite grown.''

Vivien spoke then, as if rousing from a doze. "Governess," he murmured. *"Governess?"*

Ermyntrude gave the rakehell no high marks for perception. "Tabby left us a note, and we set out to fetch her back."

"There!" Gus sighed, gazing up into Sir Geoffrey's handsome face. "I knew in my heart that you could not be guilty of such infamy. Oh, Geoffrey, can you ever forgive me?" Her eyes filled again with tears.

"Balderdash, m'dear! Nothing to forgive." Sir Geoffrey patted Gus's hand. "It's behind us now! Don't think of it anymore."

"If only it *were* behind us! But I fear it is not." Fear that fate might wrench her once more from Sir Geoffrey caused Gus to move closer still. "Vivien has forbidden me to see you. He will never permit our marriage to take place."

Sir Geoffrey inhaled Augusta's sweet perfume. He had missed her abominably. "To the devil with your brother! He can't stop our tying the knot. And if it's me you're going to marry, Gus, then it's me you must please!"

Lady Grey was enchanted by this masterful attitude. "Geoffrey!" she breathed.

Sir Geoffrey was equally enchanted by the worshipful expression on the pretty face turned up to him. "Gus!" said he. They leaned toward each other. An ardent embrace was clearly imminent, once Lady Grey's bonnet was got out of the way.

Vivien cleared his throat. "Apparently I owe you an apology, Elphinstone." Sir Geoffrey was willing to concede this was so. Solemnly, the gentlemen shook hands.

Considering that she had neatly tidied up the confusion, Ermyntrude set out toward the inn. "Osbert! Osbert, there is apparently to be no duel. Now you may pay attention to me, if you please!"

It was obvious to Lady Gray that Ermyntrude intended

198

to lead Mr. Philpotts in search of some romantic and secluded country lane. Augusta had had a similar idea herself. But Ermyntrude promised to be a rare handful, and Gus nobly decided to start out as she intended to go on. "What an excellent notion, Ermyntrude!" she said. "Your papa and I will go along."

Margot had watched this touching scene with a certain proprietary interest. Now she turned aside. "Such a fuss!" she said briskly. "Tabby, do you go on to London, or do you return to Brighton? It is obvious that there is a place for you in Sir Geoffrey's household. As there is in mine, though it is not what you are accustomed to, perhaps."

"Not London!" Perry added hastily. "I've remembered an important engagement elsewhere!"

"Ah!" Margot regarded him. "The gentleman who is not in the petticoat line." Tactfully, she withdrew to join the muffin-stuffed rooster and shaggy dog watching Perry and Drusilla engage in a game of mumblety-peg.

Vivien had come to stand beside Tabby. She avoided meeting his gaze. Of course she could not go home with her mama to that little house in North Street, where Vivien would be forever underfoot. Or if not that house, because it belonged to Sir Geoffrey, then another of a similar sort. Tabby had no illusions; she had seen how he looked at Margot. "It was good of you to come, as you thought, to my rescue!" she said stiffly. Then she realized he might have mistaken her meaning. "Of course, I knew it was on Mama's account.

Vivien quirked a brow. "Mama?"

So Margot had not told him all her secrets. "How silly of me! What can I have been thinking of? I meant Margot!" Tabby said weakly.

Vivien had scant interest in Margot just then. He sat down beside Tabby on the bench and took her hand.

"What a great many misunderstanding we have had between us—Miss Nevermind."

Would the man flirt with her now, practically under her mama's nose? Tabby was very disappointed in him. Yet she remained far from immune to his charm. "You must not speak so to me," she said gruffly. "It is not kind."

"Ah, but I have no desire to be kind to you!" Vivien put his fingers beneath her chin and tilted up her face. "You have misled me grievously—and caused me to make a fool of myself. Why the devil didn't you tell me who you were, so that we might have avoided this blasted comedy of errors?"

"What was there *to* tell you?" countered Tabby. "That I was a mere governess? Frankly, sir, I was enjoying the flirtation too much to bring it to an end!"

Vivien's restless fingers stilled. "The flirtation?" he asked.

"I know you were only amusing yourself," Tabby reassured him. "And I do not hold it against you. Indeed I am grateful, because no one had ever flirted with me before."

"No?" Vivien's grasp tightened on her wrist. "Nor will again, I assure you!"

It was no more than she had expected. Still, Tabby eyed him curiously. "Was I so very poor at it, then? Oh, you refer to the fact that I am a governess. Well, yes, I thought so myself!"

"The devil with your governessing!" snapped Vivien, so violently that Tabby stared. "That won't matter to anyone who loves you, my girl!"

"It won't?" Tabby found this difficult to believe. Still, Vivien had greater knowledge of the world than she. "Perhaps—"

"Will you be quiet?" snapped Vivien. "No one else will flirt with you because I shan't allow it! I intend to reserve all your future flirting for myself."

200

Tabby's lips suddenly felt dry. "Oh! But I have already told you that I cannot—"

"Don't remind me that I made you an improper offer!" Vivien said wryly. "It is something that I am trying very hard to forget. This is a very difficult proposal, and you are making it no easier. Despite my reputation, I am not in the habit of offering my hand and heart."

How vulnerable he looked. Tabby's throat tightened until she was barely capable of speech. "You cannot be serious."

"Can I not?" Vivien grasped her other hand, held them both against his chest. "Tabby, I have known many women, and I have never wished to marry anyone but you."

Tabby could not believe her good fortune. Or perhaps it was her accursed luck. Because, of course, she could not marry Vivien, though it might be her dearest wish. "You don't understand! I am the daughter of—"

"Oho! Margot! I thought I heard your voice." St. Erth, in an obvious good humor, had returned outside. "Stafford charged me with yet another message for you, which I quite forgot about! Not that it signifies; they are all the same. He says that he is very sorry he was such a beast, and wishes that you will come home."

"Ah, Stafford." Truth be told, Margot was growing a trifle weary of the single life and of being poor. "Tell me, St. Erth, do you truly think the duke has reformed?"

The viscount laughed. "Of course not, and neither have you. But he won't hear of a divorce. Stafford wants you back, Margot. He is willing to forgive and forget. Can you not be as generous? It's been a year since you separated and went your separate ways."

Yes, and she had newly discovered maternal instincts to consider. Margot smiled at the viscount. "Perhaps you are correct."

"What you are is the daughter of a duchess, it would

201

seem!'' murmured Vivien. "Oh, yes, I guessed—belatedly!—that Mrs. Quarles is your mama. Or Lady Stafford,
as it seems we must call her. You must tell me how that
came about. But not at this particular moment, please!''
He enfolded Tabby in a warm embrace.

They were interrupted yet once again. "Vivien!" came
an all-too-familiar female voice. With reluctance, Tabby
opened her eyes. It was indeed the divine Sara. Tabby
supposed the actress would call her horrid names again.
She braced herself.

But Sara—who knew quite well on which side her bread
was buttered and who had additionally received a most
handsome parting gift from Mr. Sanders—merely took St.
Erth's arm. "What a surprise to see you here! Have you
also ridden out to inspect some supposedly prize horse-
flesh?'' Her gaze rested on Tabby. "Ah, I see you have
not! We must interrupt you no longer. Hallo, Margot! You
here, too? Come, my dears, I have it on very good authority that there is some excellent French brandy to be
had within!''

Stunned by such forbearance, Tabby stared after the actress. "She recognized me; I know she did!''

Vivien gently turned her back to face him. "You need
not concern yourself about Sara. We have parted on good
terms. Indeed, I have apparently already been supplanted
in her affections. Still, you hesitate. My darling, what
must I do to persuade you that I have reformed?''

"Well," Tabby said judiciously, "I rather think that you
might kiss me again.''

Mr. Sanders was pleased to do so. Some moments
passed. "Oh, Vivien!" Tabby sighed when he allowed her
to draw breath. "I do love you so very much!'' and after
that pretty declaration, of course Vivien had no choice but
to kiss her once again.

Scandalous Romance

from Regency

and Maggie MacKeever